THEUNDENIABLES.ORG

(we write)

Title by Narinda Heng, excerpted from "Letter to Edren T. Sumagaysay."

Special thanks to Mike Daily for inspiration of WWI & WWII, from his book *Valley* (Bend Press, 1998).

Cheers to the Corner Booth, 1st and Central, LA, CA.

www.theundeniables.org

ISBN 978-0-578-01165-3

Dedicated to everyday writing.

TABLE OF CONTENTS

Narinda Heng

Allan G. Aquino

Helen Kim

Tani Ikeda

Tony Francesconi

{ who the hell do we think we are }

NARINDA HENG

Letter to Edren Sumagaysay

<u>06 June 2008, 11:59 pm</u>

Thank you for the letter.
Yeah, I do get it.
We're on the edge of something. Something revolutionary.

Who the hell do we think we are? Vagabond writers, trying to let people choose what they want to read and buy and put on their shelves instead of using a marketing department to convince people that they want us? Flaying ourselves out there in all of our imperfection, letting people into us and reminding them that getting paid for something doesn't mean it has real value, and not getting paid for something doesn't mean it's valueless.

The way that reality TV and gossip websites seem to be taking over the mainstream makes it feel like it's hopeless to write at all. We start to hide away in notebooks, or we stop trying to weave stories altogether because we start thinking in terms of how we would never be able to make a living from it.

I think we get so disheartened by that reality that we start to give up on writing a little bit, and focus on those careers that they give us aptitude tests for in school. The problem with those damn aptitude tests was that my results were always all over the place, and I never even felt like I needed to take those tests because I always knew that I was a writer, even if it would never be something I could put on a resume, even if I'd never cash a single check in my life for writing (not that I wouldn't love to). That I'd do whatever else it was I had to do to survive, and I'd write. Writing and living are the same thing for me. It's hard to explain that to people.

It's hard to explain to people why I get the urge to put into words all these thoughts in my brain, or to write in a blog to friends and, often, strangers. It's hard to explain to people why the words are important to me. You know what I mean. I'm sure you've had to explain to people what all that means, what it feels like when you say that you're a writer and writing is important to you but no, you're not published (yet); no, you don't work for a magazine; no, you're not trying to be a journalist; and no, you're not going to go to an MFA program so that you can buy the time to hone your craft. And we still keep writing, here, there, everywhere, because no matter what we say about how people don't value literature anymore, *people are reading*.

So here we are using the resources available to us to get our work out there, our words out there, making our brains available to people, taking them along with us in our process and hoping that it'll start them on their own. Their own path to whatever it is they want, even if it's just a side thing, an after-work hobby.

That's really what I care about, as much as telling the stories. I care about teaching people to nurture the passion in their lives. That's what you've been doing to me with the motivational email you send. I've been a member of this workshop for less than a month and the fire that was already burning inside me feels like it's blazing now.

Maybe being a writer isn't the main thing for all of *The Undeniables*, but I know that somehow, all of us believe in writing, in this process, as a way of becoming Undeniable to whatever it is we want to do.

Whatever the next phase might bring, I'm ready for it.

Peace & love & fire,
Narinda

The Arrangement (Excerpt One)

The young man tucked his pack of Marlboro Reds neatly into his front shirt pocket. He smoothed back his hair. Today would be a big day, he decided; today I am going to meet the woman I will marry.

The sun's heat beat persistently through the clouds on the warm, Long Beach morning as Veasna drove his shiny gray pickup to the home of his soon-to-be bride. A nervousness welled up in him as his fingers tapped the steering wheel in time to country music from his radio. At stoplights, the bluegrass tunes would drift from his car and passersby would look at him with a mixture of surprise and amusement, expecting a redneck but instead seeing a thin, Asian man in a pressed, plaid shirt.

—

At the house on Cherry Street, Jenny glared into the mirror as her mother chattered while expertly inserting bobby pins into her hair. She was creating some sort of ridiculous masterpiece of twists, in order to impress the young man whom Jenny would meet that day.

"I don't understand why you are going to so much trouble. It's like you're preparing for the wedding already."

"Need to make a good impression," her mother replied. "We want to make sure he likes you, don't we?"

"We also don't want to look like you're so desperate to get rid of me. He'll know there's something wrong with me."

"There's nothing wrong with you!"

Jenny's mother ended this line of conversation with a particularly sharp motion of the next bobby pin. The unspoken discussion made the air between them heavy, burdensome. It was at least an hour until Veasna was due to arrive, enough time for the dust to settle on this moment of tension. Jenny sat patiently while her mother finished the last of her task. The unsaid weighed against her, and she stared at her hands folded in her lap, resignation closing her eyes.

—

Veasna stepped out of the truck, leaving his pack of cigarettes in the glove compartment. It wouldn't do for his prospective parents-
14

in-law to reject him based on this, one of his very few vices, before they could evaluate his character. They would have to know, eventually, but hopefully not until after they decided that he would be a suitable husband for their daughter.

"Jenny," he said to himself, remembering the name that his friend had given him of the available bride. Without parents to seek a wife for him, he had been left to his own devices. At thirty-two, he had decided it was time for him to start a family, to have a few children who would carry on his legacy in this country.

He knew he was probably too old to consider himself an orphan anymore – his parents would have died sooner or later, but he couldn't help feeling somehow stranded in life without them. He had taken care of himself somewhat easily in the last ten years – he'd moved to a new country, found work, contacted his relatives at respectable intervals to report on his whereabouts and his progress. None, however, were close enough to offer to find him a wife, nor could he bring himself to ask.

Whether it was pride or shyness or both, he had never been able to consider any of his relatives qualified to find him a wife. He feared whoever they chose would be some sort of wilting-blossom type, that he would have to coddle and teach to live in the U.S. He didn't even consider marrying someone who wasn't Cambodian – there would simply be too much to explain, alter, adapt. He did not want life to be boring, nor did he want it to be a chore.

And so he began, quietly, mentioning to his friends that he was looking for an American-born, or at least "Americanized," *Khmer* woman. The catch was that she had to be willing to have an arranged marriage – the fact that she would allow her parents to choose a spouse for her would show that she had not strayed too far from tradition. This way they would be able to have a combination of the old, and the American, ways. There would be the excitement of new discoveries together, without the difficulty of one being too far ahead of the other.

The details were all laid out, the only problem being that such a girl was incredibly difficult to find. It was nearly two months before he heard anything at all. His friends were incredulous at his requirements – they did not believe that such a girl actually existed, or if she did, they did not expect her to even be within the state.

As Veasna walked toward the front door of the house on Cherry Street, he hoped that he would find this "Jenny" agreeable, and she him.

{ who the hell do we think we are }

P.T.L.D.

I would like to know once again
the clear joy in hearing a lover's voice,
without question, without apprehension.

Perhaps I suffer from posttraumatic love disorder,
unable now to walk easily into wanting,
too afraid of harming or being harmed.

There is no way to correct this,
no switch to be flipped,
there is only waiting.

There is still life in waiting,
in seeing beauty and not reaching for it,
in feeling tenderness and keeping it quiet.

The Arrangement (Excerpt Two)

Veasna pulled his truck into the driveway of his small bungalow apartment. The bungalows in the complex were small and somewhat worse for wear, but the occupants did not let that stop them from planting a few rose bushes and the succulents known as "prosperity plants." The mythology around the plants was that they could bring wealth and good fortune to whomever possessed them, but the plant must have been acquired through theft: the small seedlings that sprout beside the parent plant must be spirited away without the owner's knowledge. Veasna thought it strange that a myth should promote stealing wealth that way, but in order to be respectful, he made sure to take one of his neighbor's tiny, young plants and add it to the small plot near his own doorstep. The neighbor noticed it and came to ask him about it, and Veasna feigned ignorance about its providence, as the myth also entailed. A cheerful participant in this dance, the neighbor put on his sternest face and gave a mumbled scolding before turning on his heel and returning to his apartment.

While many of the little plots did contain plants for decorative purposes, even more of them contained compact kitchen gardens. Since the complex was occupied solely by *Khmer* people, Veasna could recognize many of the herbs lining the pavement: stalks of lemon-grass came up past his thighs; thick patches of mint spread wildly across some plots; and tall Thai basil plants, which had beautiful, tiny purple and white flowers. In the evening, when the herbs were picked for cooking, their scents permeated the air, gently perfuming it before the heavier scents of *Khmer* curries and soups and stir-fried dishes wafted into the courtyard.

Veasna had lived in this same complex since leaving his aunt's home, five years earlier. There was no real need for him to go, since he had been on amicable terms with both his aunt and his uncle-in-law, but he had wanted a quiet place of his own, where he would not feel like a burden to their family. Their four children were getting older, and he could sense that whatever extra space they had would soon be taken up by the blooming adolescents.

He had driven past this place on the way home from the factory and called the number later that evening. Within a week, he had signed a lease and begun his move.

It had been strange making a home by himself. He couldn't think of very many other *Khmer* men who lived alone. Unlike in

American culture, it was very much normal for *Khmer* children to live with their parents well into adulthood, until marriage took them to homes of their own. To create a home alone, without a family or even a wife, had made him feel unbalanced. Eventually, he became more accustomed to the quiet and to being alone, but he still missed the sound of family around him.

He had spent more weeks than he cared to admit just sitting on his linoleum floor to have dinner, and on his 1970's-style carpet to watch the small television set that his aunt and uncle had given him as a moving gift. Eventually, he found a suitable, small dining set and a couch to sit at, and the television came to sit in a laminated particle-board entertainment center.

Nearly five years later, the entertainment center was still mostly bare, save for the television set. The small cabinet above the television housed framed photographs of his parents and grandparents. A small box of red candles and a box of long incense sticks sat nestled next to a small ceramic pot, which held the ends of all of the incense that he had burned. Veasna was careful to mark his calendar for the important Buddhist holy days on which he was to light incense and provide an offering to the small altar, usually a small plate of fruit. On the anniversaries of their passing, however, Veasna would go to a *Khmer* restaurant and pick up a special roast duck or pork or chicken for the altar. Those offerings only stayed there for a few hours at most, after which the food could be consumed under the assumption that the spirit diners had already had their share.

Upon opening the cabinet after his visit to the house on Cherry Street, Veasna took note of how gray with ash the rice in the ceramic pot had become. He was tempted to replace it, but that would mean removing the ends of all the incense sticks he had burned. *Better to just let it be,* he decided.

Thinking about Jenny, *Huoung,* Veasna lit a new incense stick and held it between his palms as he bowed his head three times. He wanted to tell his parents about his decision, and to request their blessing.

—

The young woman inside the house on Cherry Street lay on her bed and stared at the ceiling, thinking about the young man whom she had just met, and the lover she had abandoned. She kept her cellular phone nearby, and attempted to convince herself that she was not waiting for another phone call, or for some force of nature to show her that it would be okay to run away.

The trouble with waiting for a sign is that while you wait, the moment to do what you wanted to do slips away.

{ who the hell do we think we are }

Whisper, 2

I whisper
the secrets
she longs to hear
when I know
she is not listening;

I am afraid,
and it is
safer
this way.

ALLAN G. AQUINO

Lakeview Elegies (Twenty): 'Eternal Sins'

TO: vincent garcia sintal
FR: arnulfo jakob, lakeview terrace asylum

hello again, mr. sintal
        we absolutely share common experiences. spiritually and
otherwise.
        some background… my grandfather became a catholic, and
that's more or less been the spiritual front yard for we jakobs 'til now.
catholic grammar and high schools for me, naturally.
        i remember bible stories. magnificent stuff, if you indulge it
fantastically. (i loved tolkien since i was a boy, and wasn't surprised
to find out that he was catholic.)
        jesus stories were always awesome. i suppose i've always had
a healthy dose of common sense, so i'm incapable of taking anything
'religious' too seriously. fairytale or note, jesus is a character;
miracles aside, he's the archetypal ghost-man.
        he goes from his preteens to his thirties in the gospels. if only
someone wrote something about his teenhood (a task i'd entertained a
while back).
        when did he discover masturbation? did he ever play doctor
with his fellow playmates, and did he ever harbor confusion if he'd
eyed another boy's naked body? natural, non-evil things – after all,
it's only a real sin if one is conscious of the wrongness of a given
action. if he at, say, age 10 had an erection at the sight (or thought) of
a naked boy or girl, wouldn't that make him as human as anybody?
divine *and* human, right? wholly divine *and* human, so dogma dictates
– but *human*, and all that entails.
        how did jesus react to his first wet dream? what did his parents
tell him when he inquired where babies come from? did his mom tell
him, 'well, you just magically appeared in my tummy,' and did he
counter-ask, 'is that how everybody gets born?', to which she blushed
and turned away.
        just how did he come to the edification that everyone should
'turn the other cheek?' did he ever have an impulsive interlude when
somebody lay his hands on him in some aggressive way, inducing him
to slug him or push him away with the intent to fuck him up? did he
clench his fist, draw back, then realize 'no, better not?'

22

and then there's his believed death. you know, i get a kick out of the gnostic take – that the crucifixion was a hoax, that some sorry sucker took his spot on the cross while he fled to france, fucked around with magdalene, and spawned the merovingians. (whatever.)

but, i mean: what if he were beheaded instead of crucified? would catholics pray before sculpted images of his body holding his head, sleepy hollow-style? what kind of fucked-up jewelry would the devout wear around their necks? or, what if jesus was lynched, a la judas? would catholics pray to and wear images of a neckbroken corpse dangling from a noose?

if rifles existed during jesus' time, would catholics pray to a corpse full of gaping, bile-oozing wounds with tissue matter scattered about like confetti? mass would be far more appealing if beer and chicharrones transubstantiated during the eucharist (ha, ha!).

and then there's the thought of jesus being castrated or drawn and quartered. what, come lent's first sunday, pray to his left arm? second sunday, right foot? come holy week, pray to his colon and scrotum?

you see, dearest vincent, most penny-dozen dullards would regard my thoughts with fiery, unforgiving judgment. when i wonder such wonders, i do not do so to be disgusting or offensive. i'm just honestly curious.

well beyond the walls of this asylum, people of the world entire do well to dismiss people like me on such terms. right, wrong, pathological – could it be that these are mere matters of popular opinion and animal conformity?

i know where i stand with everything. i'm guilty, catholicwise, of the eternal sins: 'despair,' 'presumption,' 'obstinancy,' and whatever else. (well, if i were raised calvinist it'd be a different story).

and it's not like an award, scholarship, or building would ever be named after me, in honor of whatever 'right' things i've done

but it's all a matter of opinion. when all's done, i'll roam the universe unfettered, well past the eyes and claws of stupidity.

true poetry, wouldn't you agree, maestro?

sincerest will-wishes,
arnie

{ who the hell do we think we are }

Lakeview Elegies (Twenty-Two): 'Dream of Destiny'

FR: Arnulfo Jakob, Lakeview Terrace Asylum

Oh yes, Maestro, I'm quite familiar with Jose Garcia Villa's work!

His life alone is worthy of epic interest. How he made language his own, and how few of us could aspire to such revolutionary boldness.

Anyway, as per your request, I'll share what details I remember.

Most people, so I'm told here, dream in black and white. Generally, we don't remember most of our dreams.

Well, I remember most of mine, and I dream in vivid color. Mine are especially sensual – I experience scents, skin-sensations (My wet dreams are doozies). Heart-rattling anxieties, too.

In this dream I'm calm. I appear at the head of a passageway betwixt endlessly stretching ten-foot high walls. The figure I assume's some high-ranking devil is custodian of the entry. The sky is a deep Kool-Aid-red. Blackish steam or smoke mists all around.

I remember the devil as faceless. yet, not. I remember a tallish figure, stocky, this close to obese. Thick, muscular forearms. A lumpy, smashed-in body. Man-like, yet, not. A form that'd been gnarled by irradiation or poisoning, maybe.

It grabs my right forearm, place of my tattoo. He scans my black mark with some device, like a store cashier's scanner. There's a sharp, electronic boop. The devil pushes my arm away. It glances at me with its custard eyes and utters, 'no. uh-uh.'

I don't remember if anything else happened, I just know I report to hell only to be told I'm not welcome there. The entire time, I feel no terror, just a mundanity, when I'm bathing or eating alone.

At any rate, this one dream involves my thoughts so much I try to bring it up in group talks. Nothing but indifference from all the others.

And so I wonder, of what use is prayer for the (so-called) spiritual? Do they pray to kiss god's divine ass, per material hopes? Do they pray out of want or out of reverence? Shit. I figure if you pray, you should pray to get rid of what you don't need. The grace to, little by little, gradually and steadily, free yourself of your own filth, delusions, and alienating, existential bullshit.

24

Really, I say fuck all. Religion is nothing more than tomorrow's mythologies today. One day, these superstitions will bore high school kids.

Anyway, thanks for reading and psychically listening.

A.J.

P.S.

My tattoo is 'love' in Sanskrit, a nod to Villa's 'The Anchored Angel'. I got it literally a month before the hell-dream.

{ who the hell do we think we are }

Lakeview Elegies (Twenty-Four)

TO: Percival Sintal
CC: K.E. Gein, C. Gein
FR: Vincent Garcia Sintal

This letter was from about a month before his passing…

~Vincent

***

TO: Vincent Garcia Sintal
FR: A. Jakob, L.V.T.A.

'And the worms croll out and the maggots crawl in/as the germs play blackjack on your chin.'

That was one of the first poems I ever wrote. I was around nine when I wrote it. Color me darkly, but I think the spelling errors make the verse more charming than creepy.

Mr. Sintal, I've yielded and taken the pills they've given me. In lieu of bed rest, I've requested they leave me be here in the activity room, where I can write and relax, so long as I'm not tearing up anything or anybody.

I don't know what or how I'm supposed to feel. Christ, this is weird. My head is light, yet not. I wish I knew how to describe what I feel. I'm writing so slowly. Or at least it feels that way. Meditatative…

I tell you, this place is a hellish genius. The whiteness of everything blinds 'n distracts from the unsubtle bleach and Lysol, the B.O. of the orderlies, the biley reek of the droning internees.

The worst kind of horror story. The esoteric psychic, melancholic terrorism. This place is a masterpiece of forced coercion. Worst of all, I still don't know, and perhaps might never know, why I'm here.

That 'slot machine world'-feeling is coming. Khrist, even the Zodiac Killer had more graceful handwriting than mine.

Gein, that fucking idiot. His eyeball hovers about like a mosquito, sneaking peeks at me while I write this. Cannot believe how violent this place makes me feel.

I am the easiest man to loathe. Despite my education, despite my intelligence, despite whatever manners or dignities I bear: I am a tall man of color with a shaved head and, were I not in these damned flimsy patients' robes, dressed in casual, baggy clothing. I embody the archetypal American monster.

They're as dense and sedated as cattle, the potato-heads surrounding me. They're cut from the same rag as those millions who tremble stupidly when they get wind of another bogeymanish al jazeera video. Bin Laden makes them shit because growing multitudes deify him – and understandably so.

Fuck all that. Listen: I know danger. I know brutality. And when someone wants to do something to you, they DO it. They don't send you a Betamax of their bug-eyed self going, "yeah, it's me, and I'll fuck you up when I see you." No!

If we, damned but communal as we are, endure pressure from multiple sources while they, those devil-on-high feel pressured by the evils they'd propagated… then I'm wondering, to what degree is my own paranoia justified?

This goddamned medication has nothing to do with how I feel or who I am, or will/might be. I was not "born" this way…

~A.

Lakeview Elegies (Twenty-Five): 'Last Sent In Life'

TO: Vincent Garcia Sintal
FR: Arnulfo Jakob, L.V.T.A.

Thank you, Poesia – I'm beyond grateful. Thanks. I can't imagine why you'd keep my letters, but I thank you for the validation I'd find no place else in the world entire.

You need not tell me what the others say when they write you. The Geins in particular, I don't care to know their thoughts – I know what they are, and that's enough.

While I don't know why I'm here – this purgatorial septic tank – it is clear to me why *they're* here. Perhaps the Gein lads and I need each other to validate each other's self-absorption. They remind me that I'm light-years past their rotten apple imaginations. I remind them how normal they think they are. They're here to feel more human (though pathetically so).

The Geins are a generation away from possum-eating, cousin-screwing idiots whose lives revolved around butter churning, waxing Grampa Wilford's pickup, gulping potato vodka, and mediating, by way of Winchesters, arguments over who sodomized whose chickens. Their G.E. degrees and pretenses at literacy won't ever bury their lowliness.

Have you ever read their writing? The bastards started writing poetry because they got into you, and my stuff, as well. Copernicus writes bullshit about love and longing ("honey trees" are the best image he conjures) then parades his filth as if he's a demigod who created a new civilization. He reminds of a potty-training two-year-old who exclaims, "Mama, look, look!" after he drops his first shit-log into his parents' toilet.

My sympathies and condolences if ever they mailed you their, whatever you want to call them, "poems."

Anyway – per your request, I'll write you about my teaching experiences. I'll need time to recharge my mind and properly recollect…

Ta,

Arnie

Lakeview Elegies (Addendum): 'Excerpts from Hypnotherapy Transcriptions'

TO: V.G. Sintal
FR: Arnulfo Jakob, L.V.T.A.

Here it is. I'm not ashamed but, I swear, I remember none of this.

**

Lucid dream. Awful... replay. I wake up in my bed. That *fuck* is asleep next to me, pressed to me. His... [clears throat] *shit*-breath smells... gin. Snores, 'basso-profundo!' Scary. 'His eyes twitter open. Pinkish. He grins. Gropes my crotch [gasp]. Shushes me [sighs], squeezes me like a soft tomato. He draws his stubbly face [sighs], kisses me. I'm screaming inside. Fuckin' sleep paralysis [coughs], alien fuckin' abduction. He, he... slathers, stinking *spit* all over my face. Shit is real, shit is *too* goddamn real!

**

He's in our kitchen. Watching another Laker game. Munches leftovers. So I'm creeping up. I'm, ah... I'm... like a hawk, fixed on the back of his head. No sound. Nah. I got this, this linoleum knife in my hand, my right hand, got, like, an icepick. I... swoop up, blood-choke with my left arm! *Superman* grip! Then, one move, plunge the blade into his gut! *Balls deep!* [clears throat, cough] draw it... 'cross, steadily. *Blood... splats* like a water-balloon. Guts're... wormy. Ooze out like a Twinkie. He's hot. Shaking.

I sip his pain. [scoffs] Blood... of the new and everlasting covenant! He, uh, he... he... [smacks lips] he... he tastes [snickers]... *exquisite!* [laughs]

~ A.

HELEN KIM

Creation

Some are weak, he said. Not like the old man down the street who is physically weak, too feeble to carry his own simple groceries any longer, but in mind and spirit. And though the old man moves at a pace for a snail, he is more admirable than the mentally weak man because the body often atrophies quicker than the mind. The weak-minded atrophy at an early age, through misuse and poor handling (as if this reminder was a secret!), added the fact that brain cells do not rejuvenate. We must be disdainful of the weak minds, he said, as if it were contagious.

This is one of many opinions I heard from the man on the corner stop. I, just a simple street pigeon, grey in color with white specks (quite beautiful, some say), came to his acquaintance only after many months of annoyance: he gladly ravaged up pieces of bread, torn from silly American tourists' baguettes, for his own mouth.

Thank goodness he was not like the man before him, who licked his finger moist and soaked up all leftover crumbs like a sponge: we nearly starved. Even the crumbs in the dirt between the cobblestones! That was the tragic spring that we never mention, for it brings back bad memories of shameful and drastic measures.

It's natural to be offended at the overriding and widespread assumptions that pigeons are stupid, lazy, and fat. Most adolescent pigeons go through a period of anarchy and physical dissent, usually characterized by shitting everywhere they sit. Trees, people– even Renaissance-period cathedrals—it doesn't matter.

As a whole, we've accepted man's low expectations and negative impressions by casting this stereotype off as an unfortunate misunderstanding due to the lack of human brain cell regeneration.

I was not sure of the corner man's diatribe about weakness and brain cells. We believe we are the incarnations of clouds, crying rain in longing to reach Earth. Once on Earth, we fly upwards, in an attempt to reach the sky we miss—a lovely cyclical creation myth. Because we are incarnates, our sole tenet is that our souls and minds pass to our worldly pigeon bodies. The idea that cells were unable to go through rejuvenation was absolutely repulsive.

Utility

   "You can't give everyone everything at once– there's the
diminishing utility law. It might be great at first, whatever it is you
want or have– money, sex, toys, sex toys– but it won't be that great
after a while. It can't. It's because you never had anything at first.
You go from broke. Go for broke. So it's always the best, no matter
what. Remember when you lost your virginity? Then 25 years later.
You feeling it the same? Nope. But that's how the world works,
human nature, the law of diminishing utility, returns. You live and let
live. Can't do nothing, but try to pretend like you've had nothing and
it's all spick-span new."
   Roy finished mumbling to himself, his flushed face settling
nicely in his plate of cold nachos, his dessert after a buffet of beers.

Drinks

She seemed friendly enough, but who's not, at a bar? Well–
lots of girls– they give you the snotty bitchy look as if they didn't shit–
but it was some type of innate behavior girls put on when they wear
red lipstick and smutty-slutty heels, as if it's the sealing accessory to
their perfect outfit. She was a brunette, holding a blue drink and a red
clutch, and seemed nice enough. We chatted; she commented on the
weather these days. (Cloudy with hints of rain.) I asked her if I might
be able to call her another time and she told me she might be the last
person in the world who didn't have a phone; she was rebelling. I
thought of the indigenous tribes I'd read about in National Geographic.
Surely they didn't have phones. She didn't offer any other contact and
typical, awkward silence ensued.

I asked her what she was drinking. "Adios, Motherfucker," she
answered, laughing.

Coffee

      Jack's legs dangled over the long pier. He'd been sitting there for a while, since the sun traveled from one end to the other, hovering over his pale legs and a glassy pool of moss. Since forever he wanted to move to the city but he was there—she was there—and there was not the city—so he stayed.

      Two cups of coffee never hurt anybody, he thought—and turned around to reach for his pot and drank one more cup, straight up black, no cream and no sugar and he heard her coming. She sat next to him in silence and a breeze. Tossed her hair and dipped long legs into the lake, until the sun reached its evening residence. Good-Night, he said.

TANI IKEDA

{ who the hell do we think we are }

Bonsai People

Strange tree
Growing in the sand

Crooked lines
In the mess halls

Barbed wire taught
Branches where to grow

Twisting their bodies
In the heat

The weight
Of their roots carried

Hundreds of people
Into rows of pots

TONY FRANCESCONI

{ who the hell do we think we are }

faces

a face drips down off your face
puddles up on the desk below
with the ashes, wood, paper, and smoke
just a slow trickle of flesh melting away
a pool forms below and begins to reflect
within the warped face looking back there appeared an entrance
it was marked by a glowing understanding of one's self
step through and suddenly you're confronted
by the angry comments thrown about that day
you're staring face-to-face with regret
who tells you that he's pointless
this place seems so familiar
almost like church
a little like a warm day
but most likely
it's just tears

dripping

retarded development of human skills
progressive development within movement
blank stares aren't blank
keep watching
gnashing of skin
slapping of tails
crooked grind, boned-out grab
flow, slow, long, grrrrallp
flip it one-eighty shove-it the rest
stand on the edge of your destiny
the only thing you know is what's next
you drop in
everything else fades away
push the last bit of energy into the next thing,
the only thing.

life drips off your nose
onto the deck,
through the grip,
and down within
those stress cracks
that formed long ago.

{ who the hell do we think we are }

Monday wrong bus...

bus, again...
caught in a time-trap
one wife and countless girlfriends later

You ever question that shit?
I did, do, don't anymore.

Those weird years that made you question.
All of that work, gone. But you aren't.

As if you'd been immersed in glue,
You used to swim through colored oil.

Then you cut to: Waiting For The Bus... Again.
Refreshing cold in your eyes.
You're here now, funny as it seems.
One down, 4 to go...

rolling meadows

stone fucking monoliths
six maybe seven of them
and that cell tower looks so goddamn lonely
all breaking the horizon line of trees
rippled residential roofs
microscopic bloodstream full of cars
slow-motion, white noise
all goes unheard
in the morning

{ who the hell do we think we are }

storytime...

there was this guy named Beef Chuck.
no shit? yeah fer' real.
mean parents I guess.

he lived inside an old abandoned candy factory.
stole some paint from the construction site down the way.
repainted the entire interior bright ORANGE
he would sit in there on cold winter days painting shippin' boxes
WHITE

lollipops, lemonheads, jawbreakers, all painted over clean and perfect.
when he'd finish he'd stack them, all 48 two foot boxes into a cube
4(L) x 4(W) x 4(H).
you know, cinder block structures, like the movies, you know...

he'd stand back after he built this odd cube, admiring for a good hour.
head totally clear, almost happy, the city had evaporated inside that
vibrant room.
then he'd hike up the stairs to the catwalk, 40 feet up.
walk to the ledge,
turn around,
close his eyes,
list over,

and drop.

ELAINE DOLALAS

LAUGHING THROUGH TEARS
a novella

Ch 1: Smiley Face

All it takes to bring a smile to my face is some bright sunshine, some cool shade under a tree and a clear, blue sky.

October, 2002. While walking to class, my cell phone rings.
PRIVATE NUMBER

Normally, that means it's my parents calling. They don't list their phone number, which makes caller I.D. on my cell phone pointless.

"Mom?"

There's no one on the other end. I hang up. My cell phone rings again.
PRIVATE NUMBER

Again?

"Hello? Mom?! Are you there?!" No one replies. I hang up again.

Annoyed, I continue walking to class. My cell phone rings again, only this time I recognize the number. It's my aunt.

"Diane? What's your dad's number at work?" she asks with a strange tone. There's panic in her voice, but she's trying to cover it up with a friendly tone. It's the voice she used when I was a kid when she told me my grandmother was hit by a van.

"Huh? Why?" The air feels cold. Everything feels different. I know something's wrong.

"Oh... nothing. Your *Tita* Red and I are trying to reach your mom, but she's not picking up." Everything feels false. She's covering up something.

"Ohhhkay. It's 818-410-1712."

"Thanks *dai*. Don't worry." Why did she say don't worry? Why did she call me *dai*? She hasn't called me that in years. She hasn't called me that since my grandmother's accident.

I run into a friend from class and find out our professor is out at a conference. Class is subsequently cancelled. That's one piece of good news. I feel a knot in my stomach. My aunt's odd phone call; the private number calls with no one on the other line; something is going on. I hesitantly dial home.

"Diane... I have to go outside to flag the ambulance... Your mom..."

{ who the hell do we think we are }

All I can hear is the fear in my dad's voice. I have never heard him afraid. The knot in my stomach turns into a bottomless pit of worry. I'm seventy miles away. What do I do?

I run to my car, across campus, and drive home.

I have to get home…

I wish I never went home.

Ch 2: It's Going to be Okay

It's the middle of the afternoon. There's no traffic on the 405 Freeway. I make it to the Valley in record time: Forty-five minutes. Not that the time really matters. I'm so used to the drive that I feel like anything close to an hour is a "quick" trip.

On the way to the Valley I find out my mom is at Sacred Heart Hospital, in Majestic View City.

I have no idea why the city is called "Majestic View." The city itself is flat, dry, and lower middle class. The one majestic view came from the drive-in movie theater that used to show films every night. I remember driving past it on my way to my grandmother's house. My auntie would sneak us into the drive-in by covering three of us kids with a blanket. I don't think she really pulled one over on the teenager selling her tickets. I really don't think the kid cared.

There is no more Majestic View City drive-in. It was torn down years ago to make way for a new junior high school. I didn't understand why they would build another school in the neighborhood. Across the street from the junior high school is a middle school. Two blocks up from the middle school is an elementary school. My parents never sent me to any of these schools, because there were numerous stories about kids getting kidnapped and raped in the neighborhood. If that was the case, why did they keep building schools?

I ignore the schools and head into the parking structure of Sacred Heart. My uncle meets me in the parking structure. My *Tito* Mitch is like my second dad. *Tito* Mitch and my dad are best friends. When his three sons and I were playing in his backyard, *Tito* Mitch and my dad would be drinking whiskey and beers in the garage. He flags me down. His face is calm.

"How was the drive?"

I shrug. "Eh, alright I guess."

"Your dad is with your mom. Your *Tita* Nitcole is with them." I brace for him telling me how my mom is doing. He never does.

The sliding doors open to an emergency waiting room. I slowly walk into stale air. The doors close behind me. I look back and see E.M.T.'s lifting an empty gurney into an ambulance. *Tito* Mitch guides me to my mom.

I don't recognize her. She's hooked up to machines. I don't know what they all do. They just look painful. One's helping her breathe. One's monitoring her heart. She's asleep. She doesn't look like mom.

My dad holds her hand. His tired and worried face looks up to greet me. There are no words.

I can't take it. My eyes swell. This can't be happening.

This
can't
be
happening.

She's not supposed to be in this bed. She's not supposed to be hooked up to those machines. She was on her way to a job interview. She finally had a good lead. Yesterday she had gone to morning mass. She said her prayers that her interview would go well.

This
can't
be
happening.

I can't take it. I storm out of the room. Tears flow down my face. I haven't cried this hard since my grandmother's funeral.

This
can't
be
happening
again.

I pace. The sliding doors open and close with my steps. The sound irritates me, so I sit on a nearby bench. My shoulders and knees begin to shake. I fumble in my purse, for cigarettes. I usually never smoke when my relatives are around. But fuck it.

I inhale.

The menthol calms me down, but the tears don't stop.

"You smoke?"

Tito Mitch looks at me with a disappointed eye.

"Well… this is a shitty way for you to find out." I blubber the words through my tears.

I inhale menthol. I watch the cigarette burn, as ash begins to form.

"Are you okay?" an unfamiliar voice asks. "Would you like a hardboiled egg? You were so happy when you walked in, and then you stormed out of here…"

I look up and see a kind, young black girl's face looking at me with concern. I put my hand out and accept the hardboiled egg. I forgot to eat breakfast, before heading to class. I haven't eaten all day. The egg looks perfect.

"Thank you. I guess you could say I'm having a bad day." I wipe my tears with a napkin my uncle has produced from his pocket. *Tito* Mitch has a habit of grabbing a stack of napkins everywhere he goes. For emergencies, he says. This certainly was one of them.

The young black girl squeezes my shoulder. No words need to be said. Pain is universal. I try my best to smile, and thank her with my eyes. She walks back into the waiting room. My uncle sits with me, as I finish my cigarette. I remember the smell of Marlboro Lights that used to follow him. I almost offer him a cigarette, but my *Tita* Nitcole pats me on the back.

"*Susmariyoseph!*"

A phrase I've heard her say a thousand times before. Jesus. Mary. Joseph.

"Smoking?!"

I look up at her and sigh. I exhale loudly and put out my cigarette in the ashtray next to me. I roll the hardboiled egg on the arm of the bench and begin to peel the shell. I try to peel large pieces of eggshell. I've always gotten annoyed by little pieces.

"Is she going to be okay?" I ask as I bite into the egg.

"Let's go inside…" She wants me to be with my dad.

"I can't. Is she going to be okay?" The sight of my mom hooked up to all those machines frightens me.

"They're going to move her to K.P. Woodland Hills. The C.C.U. floor." She stares off into space as she says these words. My eyes and ears can't believe what I'm hearing. K.P. Woodland Hills? C.C.U. floor?

"Isn't that the floor *Lola* was on?" I can't mask the fear in my voice.

"You should really go inside and stay with your mom. Your dad is tired." She doesn't answer my question. She can't answer my question. She's still battling with the idea of her sister being on the same floor her mother was on, years ago.

"Come on, *dai*. Let's go in." *Tito* Mitch's calming voice soothes me for a moment.

I throw the half eaten egg in the trash. I walk in the door and meekly smile to the young black woman. I wonder who she's waiting for. I hope she's okay. My dad is talking to someone about my mom's transfer. I go to him and grab his hand. I haven't held his hand since I was a child. Tears well up in his eyes. Tears well up in mine. My *Tita* Nitcole holds my mom's hands. My *Tito* Mitch pulls out a rosary and begins to pray.

"I believe in God. The Father Almighty. Creator of Heaven and Earth..."

I try to mouth the words, but nothing comes out.

I look at my feet. In my hurry to get to class, I didn't notice I'm wearing mismatched socks. One red argyle sock. One blue striped sock. Tears begin to fall. I laugh at my feet. I don't bother wiping them away. I laugh through my tears.

"Our father who art in heaven..."

I squeeze my father's hand.

"hallowed be thy name..."

I laugh at my feet.

"thy kingdom come..."

I look at my mom.

"thy will be done..."

I begin to pray.

"on earth as it is in heaven."

Ch 3: The Waiting Room

The phone rings. I'm wide awake. My eyes are dry from crying. I'm in my bed, staring at the ceiling. *Tita* Nitcole told me to get some rest, but I couldn't sleep.

"Hello…"

My dad answers the phone. He hasn't slept either.

"Does she really need to have surgery?"

I sit up. My body tenses with worry. I fumble for my shoes. I don't even bother to turn the light on in my room. A sense of urgency fills the house. I take my seat at the dining table. There is yesterday's newspaper sitting in a pile. Mom had pulled out which coupons she wanted to cut.

"Okay. I'll be right there." *I'll* be right there?

My voice quivers.

"I'm going with you."

My dad looks at me and attempts to crack a smile. "Diane, just get some rest. *Tita* Nit-"

"I'M GOING WITH YOU."

I get up from the table and put my cell phone and wallet in my hoodie pockets. Dad stares at me and sighs. He knows I won't budge on this. I'm stubborn. Just like her.

It's around 2am. The night envelops his car as we begin the trip. K.P. Woodland Hills is next to his office. Dad doesn't need to think of the route. His hands guide the steering wheel without a second guess.

Thoughts begin to run through my head. Is she going to make it? What's going to happen? Why did this happen? Dad fumbles with his phone and calls my cousin Ted. Ted is the pride and joy of our family. He fulfilled *Lolo's* dreams of having a doctor in the family. He's extremely smart, but he has always been cold and removed.

"Ted's going to meet us at the hospital." I don't even bother looking at my dad. Tears begin to fall.

"What if she dies?" My voice cracks. How can there be more tears? Didn't I cry enough today?

Dad doesn't answer me. He concentrates on the road. The thirty-five minute drive at 7am is now a twenty minute drive at 2am. No one greets us at the parking kiosk, so we drive in and park in front of Medical Building 2.

I hate this hospital. After my grandmother's accident, she was sent to K.P. Woodland Hills, for treatment.   My parents and I would come here every weekend and sit in her room. I would try to do homework in the waiting room, but instead I would count the cars in the parking lot. Or my cousins and I would explore different floors of the hospital.

I step out of the car, into the cold night air.   We walk into the hospital; while my dad hesitates on which way to go, I retrace my childhood steps.

"It's this elevator dad…"

We enter and I push the button for the third floor. The door opens and I stare out the windows of the hallway. I can see our car. I don't remember walking, but I find myself in front of the nurses' station. A doctor hovers over my mother. My chest tightens. I can't be here.

"I'm going to be in the waiting room." I turn around and push the handicap button. The double doors open, and I walk out.

I hate this place.

I find a seat in the dark waiting room. Channel 7 is on and the repeat showing of the 11pm news ends. Someone in a studio in Burbank queues the next program. *Steven Spielberg's Hook.* Seriously? *Hook?* They have nothing better to show at two in the morning. I sit in silence and try to get comfortable in the stiff, waiting room chair. There's another woman sitting in the row of seats to my right. She looks like she's been through hell. I wonder if I look the same.

"The doctor doesn't think she needs surgery right now. They're going to run some tests and then we'll find out if she really has to have it."

I pause.

"What?"

Dad puts a heavy hand on my shoulder and sits in the seat next to me.

"Do you just wanna stay here?"

He already knows the answer. I can't bring myself to be with mom in this state and he can't be far away from her. I nod my head.

"Okay. Just keep an eye out for Ted."

Dad leaves me with Robin Williams, Julia Roberts, and Dustin Hoffman. I've seen this movie numerous times before. I hate this movie, but I can't keep my eyes from the screen. I laugh as the Lost

54

Boys chant, "RU-FI-OOOOOOOO." My heart breaks as an aged old man murmurs, "Lost, Lost, Lost." Robin Williams' Peter asks, "Lost what?" The aged old man is Toodles. "I've lost my marbles." I laugh at this out loud. I forget I'm sitting in a dark, cold waiting room.

"Hi, Diane. How are you doing?" Ted's face tells me he knows exactly how I'm doing.

"Ehh."

He takes the seat next to me. I pretend to scoot over and give him room.

"I know it's rough right now, but I want you to be prepared. Your mom might not make it. She had a pretty bad stroke."

These are not the words I want to hear right now. I stay focused on the nineteen inch screen mounted on the wall. The Lost Boys are making fun of Peter because he can't imagine the feast in front of him.

"Dad's inside with mom. She's in room 304." I can feel Ted's eyes staring at me. I'm mad. Why would you tell someone that?

"I'm going to check on your dad." Ted waits for my reaction

"Mmmm," I grunt in retort as he leaves.

"What a jerk," the woman waiting with me laughs. Our eyes meet and words don't need to fill the room.

"Thanks."

Peter finds his imagination. He fights for his son, who is dressed in a mini Captain Hook costume. Rufio gets stabbed by Captain Hook. He's dying. You can die in Neverland? Peter holds Rufio, as he exhales his last words. "You know what I wish?"

"The doctor says she needs the surgery. They're paging the neurosurgeon. He'll be here soon."

I wish I wasn't here.

Ch 4: Lola Ling

The Routine

I have always been a creature of routine. Before mom got sick my routine was typical of your normal super senior college student.

Go to class.
Avoid going to class.
Work at Borders.
Pretend to read for class.
Hang out with friends.
Smoke cigarettes while hanging out with friends.
Talk shit while smoking cigarettes while hanging out with friends.

Like I said, it was your typical super-senior college student shit. Somehow, through all the trauma, I created a routine for myself. I normalized the situation as a way to cope.

Sleep through class.
Drive to the Valley from Orange County.
Sit in mom's hospital room.
Push food around and pretend to eat something in the hospital cafeteria.
Sit in hospital waiting room with relatives who have come to visit mom.
Sit in hospital waiting room by myself, long after relatives have headed home.
Drive home.
Pull out books and plan to study.
Turn on television to Cartoon Network.
Fall asleep with T.V. on, books left untouched.

The bedroom

"What are you going to do about school?"
I rub my eyes and try to go back to sleep. There must be an episode of *Home Movies* on right now.
"*Pssst Hoy,* what are you going to do about school?!"

The hairs on my neck stand up. I don't recall *Home Movies* having an old Filipino lady as a character. I feel someone kick my leg. I must be dreaming.

"Diane! What are you going to do about school?!"

I can't ignore the voice any longer. I sit up and see a small, old Filipino lady sitting on the books I left on the foot of my bed.

"Wha? Who are you? How'd you get in here?!" I've heard enough stories from my dad about spirits haunting kids.

She smiles at me. The moonlight seeps through the curtains and causes her white hair to gleam.

"You know."

I recognize the green flowered duster she wears. I see it every time I come home.

The balikbayan box

My dad sends *balikbayan* boxes home to the Philippines, every Christmas. The boxes are filled with bags of pistachio nuts, Planter's peanuts, Ensure supplement drinks, and old clothes and shoes my dad had either outgrown or didn't want anymore. One year, he sent portraits he had taken of me. Dad framed an 8 x 11 headshot of my five year old, smiling self. My relatives called us when they received the box. Dad had me speak to people I was supposed to know and love, but had never met.

"Hi *Lola?*"

"Diane? You look so pretty in your picture! You're getting so big now, ha!"

"Thank you... here's Papa!"

I passed the phone to my dad. I didn't have anything else to say to her. I was five.

My *Tito* Nate took a picture of my *Lola* Ling with my headshot. She wore her white hair in a loose bun with glasses, a friendly smile, and a green flower print duster. It would be our only picture together.

The bedroom, cont'd

I can't believe it's her. There's no way it's *Lola* Ling. I blink twice, very hard.

"*Lola* Ling?"

She nods.

"This has to be a dream. You can't be here."

Her forehead crinkles. "And why not?"

"Well for one thing… you're dead."

"HAHA!"

Her laughter fills the quiet void of the room. I do not know how this tiny woman can have such a loud laugh. I grew up and older, but my image of her stayed the same. Small, white hair, glasses, and a green flower print duster.

"Better late than never." Her voice continues to echo in my room.

I squeeze a pillow to my chest. I think I'm going crazy. It's 1am and I'm having a conversation with my dead grandmother.

What
The
Fuck.

"You never answered my question. So what are you going to do about school?" *Lola* Ling pressures me for an answer.

I shrug my shoulders. "I dunno…"

"Diane…" She gets up and moves towards me. I feel my eyes get wider and wider. *Lola* Ling doesn't walk towards me, she floats. I know I shouldn't be afraid of her. She isn't here to hurt me. Dad always told me to not be afraid of ghosts who were not trying to hurt you. He never taught me how to tell if they were there to hurt me. His answer to that question: "You'll just know."

I knew she wasn't there to hurt me. It still scared the bejesus out of me. Dad's wrong.

"You know you have to finish. You have to get your degree. It's what your mom wanted."

The Lecture

Lola Ling is addressing a question I've been thinking about for the past couple of days. I've been avoiding class more than your average slacker. I simply do not care. I emailed my professors about my situation and they were all sympathetic to my situation. It helps that I'm finishing up my Asian American Studies degree. I finished my Film Studies degree last year. I declared Asian American Studies as my double major last year. I avoided the real world with one more year of school. Over the past four years, I've built a relationship with the Asian American Studies faculty through working with various Asian American student organizations.

And then there's Topher. Topher Li. We met in Asian Am 50A. He had a bucket cap over his head and started to snore during lecture. His snoring got so loud that I started laughing. I threw my pencil at his head. I threw small squares of paper at his hat. Pretty soon, I was using the Bear mascot on his bucket hat as target practice. My shenanigans did not go unnoticed by the professor.

"I know having an evening lecture is difficult, but I would like it if you could stay awake. That means you, Topher."

The snoring stopped and Topher shook the paper squares off his soccer jacket. He pushed his bucket cap off his eyes to reveal a younger version of Professor Li's face.

"Sorry."

He looked at the paper squares and pencils surrounding his chair.

"Is this your doing?" I feared that he'd be pissed, but he asked me with a sarcastic twinkle in his eye.

"Yup." I smiled back at him.

"Thanks. That's all I need. Getting caught sleeping in class by my dad."

Topher became my best friend in college. He was the first person I called when I found out about my mom. He told his dad about my situation, who then told the rest of the faculty. My professors decided to give me extensions on my midterms. I turned in shit papers, but still got B's. I did not want to be there. Topher could see that.

"Are you going to take a leave?" He exhaled on his cigarette, as he asked.

I inhaled on my cigarette and took a sip from my *Castleberry*, a pint with a half of Newcastle and half Raspberry Cider. We sat at our usual patio table, at our school's pub.

"I'm thinking about it…"

"You know… I'll support whatever decision you come to, but I just wanna say this. Would she really want you dropping out?" He pounded the rest of his beer.

I stare at my pint glass, avoiding his concern.

"I know…"

The bedroom, again

"I know... I know, *Lola*." I still can't believe I'm talking to my dead grandmother.

Lola Ling pinches my cheek and giggles. The scent of rose petals envelopes me.

"You're a figment of my imagination aren't you." I look in her eyes and try to get some kind of confirmation.

"I am? Can your imagination do this?" All the lights in my room turn on at once. The television and radio flicker on and off.

I squeeze my pillow tighter.

"Please stop."

The chaos stops. *Lola* Ling puts her hand on my wrist and asks me one last time.

"So, what are you going to do about school?"

Her forehead wrinkles, as she waits for my answer. I stare at the books sitting at the foot of my bed. I have to graduate. Mom's going to see me graduate. All I have to do is survive this year. If I was able to survive this week, I can survive this year.

"You know."

She squeezes my wrist and smiles.

"I do?"

I laugh and hear her laugh harmonize with mine. She whispers in my ear, "Good answer."

BUZZ
BUZZ
BUZZ
BUZZ

The alarm clock reads 8:30am.

BUZZ
BUZZ
BUZZ

Time to get ready for class.

Ch 5: Donut Star Adventures

Donut Star

It's 2am, and I'm sitting on a cold, green metal chair smoking cigarettes in front of Donut Star. Donut Star is the only thing open twenty-four hours a day, in Irvine. I've spent numerous late nights sitting on these cold, green metal chairs. Back home I would never be out at a donut shop at 2am. In Irvine I spit intellectual bullshit with friends; in the Valley I'd be avoiding stares from transients and grifters.

"Hot cocoa and chocolate donut."

Shifting in my chair causes the metal to brush against my skin. "Thanks, Topher."

"When's Noel and Will getting here?" Topher, Noel, Will, and I make up the Donut Star crew. What initially started out as a midterm study break has become a weekly tradition, for the past three years. If we aren't playing _Goldeneye_ at Will's house or watching D.V.D.'s at Topher's apartment, we can be found at Donut Star. Occasionally, other friends join us, but the four of us are the main players of the crew.

"How ya holdin' up?" Topher has gotten very big brother on me. I appreciate it, but I just don't feel like talking tonight. I sip my hot cocoa and light up a Benson and Hedges. I feel like an old Filipino man, smoking these cigarettes.

"Ehh…"

"Whattup bitches." It's Noel's usual welcome. Will tips his fitted Angels baseball cap and takes a seat.

"You go to class today, Diane?" Will and I have Filipino American history together.

The Valley

"Nah, I woke up late. The drive from the Valley took longer than usual. I was just hitting Westminster when it was 11:30." I've missed most of my Monday morning classes. I get to the Valley on Friday afternoon and head back to Irvine on Monday morning. The plan is that I wake up early and get to class on time. I usually stay at the hospital till 12am, get home by 12:30, and have a late night meal with my dad. I turn in around 1:30 or 2. Dad stays up till 3am, going

61

over mom's blood pressure notes, sipping double shots of whiskey, and catching up on the evening news. I'm not sure he really pays attention to the stories onscreen.

"You have to make sure he's healthy, Diane." *Tita* Nitcole tells me to look out for him. He hasn't been eating much. She told me that the stress is getting to him and he could be developing an ulcer.

"I know… I know…"

"You too. You should quit smoking. It's ba--" The look on my face stops her. I've inherited my mom's angry face. My mom's *sungit* face. Mom is the "mean" sister. She's not necessarily mean, but brutally, ruthlessly honest. She is the only one who can make my *Tita* Nitcole cry. When my relatives were planning my *Lola* and *Lolo's* big 50th wedding anniversary party, they were frantic with getting the details hashed out. *Tita* Nitcole and mom were on the phone having an argument that ended with phones being slammed. The next day, my cousin tells me my mom made his mom cry.

As a nurse, *Tita* Nitcole is not a big fan of smoking. When I was a kid, *Tita* Nitcole found *Tito* Mitch's carton of Marlboro Lights. She broke every cigarette in half. *Tito* Mitch found a better hiding spot, afterwards. Growing up, I never saw him without a pack of Marlboro Lights. He would keep a pack in the sun visor. I don't know why *Tita* Nitcole never took that pack away. He eventually quit, but the effects of second hand smoke had already taken us over. His oldest son and I would become smokers.

Donut Star, cont'd

"You gonna go through that whole pack tonight, missy?" Noel has never smoked a cigarette in his whole life. It would ruin his skin. A modeling scout spotted him at a volleyball game, in high school. Told him he needed to just tone and bulk up and she could get him work. Personally, I think it was a cougar hitting on a young cub. I don't think the "scout's" words ever left him. He's always been *tres* fashionable.

"Uh-huh." I let the menthol fill my lungs.

I don't pay attention to the conversation. Topher, Noel, and Will have a marathon of a conversation. The topics range from the latest digital gadgets, porn, music, Wong-Kar Wai, and how shitty school is going.

"Shit, what time is it?" Will fumbles for his phone.

"It's almost 4am." Minus the grunts and apathetic nods, those are the only words I've said all night.

"Good thing my first class is at 1pm." Noel hasn't had a morning class since freshman year.

I get up from my chair and reach for the sky. The night air brushes against my stomach. I quickly pull my hoodie down and dig my hands into my pocket.

We say our farewells. I hug Noel and Will, while Topher waves goodbye as he opens the driver's side door. I get settled in the passenger seat. It's a familiar spot. When we were freshman, Topher would pick me up from my dorm and we would go exploring. He showed me all the secret Orange County spots like Donut Star, Super K-mart in Mission Viejo, our table at Gypsy Den in Santa Ana, and a secret alcove in Laguna Beach where we would listen to the waves at midnight.

I close my eyes as he starts the engine. My hair smells like smoke, from all the cigarettes. I begin to drift off to sleep, never noticing Topher staring down at me. It's a look I've missed before. It's a look he gives when I'm not paying attention.

Topher brushes the hair out of my face, sighs, and heads home.

Ch 6: Topher's Story

I met Diane in Asian Am 50A lecture. It was the second week of class and I was dreaming about being attacked by Smurfs throwing mushrooms at me, when I heard my dad call me out about sleeping in lecture.

"I know having an evening lecture is difficult, but I would like it if you could stay awake. That means you, Topher."

The familiar tone of getting in trouble by your dad isn't welcomed in lecture. I fumbled awake in my chair to find a girl in my row snickering at my situation.

"Is this your doing?"

Her laugh filled the room; at least I thought it did. We were at a break in lecture and other kids were filing out to grab a smoke break. I got up and brushed squares of paper off my shoulders. She smiled and responded, slyly.

"Yup…"

I laughed with her and started to make my way to the aisle, brushing against her leg.

That Girl

"Wanna grab a smoke break?" I didn't know if she smoked, but practically everyone did. The lecture hall was almost empty. Another sleepy student, the Teaching Assistants, and my dad were left. She got up and we were so close we could've been slow dancing.

"Sure."

Diane was a familiar face around campus. At least, she was familiar to me. I would see her walking to campus, trekking through the music buildings. I knew she lived in *Corte Nuevo*, the residence halls behind the School of Art. I would visit my friends in *Sonido*, the fine arts hall, and see her walking into *Caballo*, the hall next door. I tried to ask my friends about her, but *Corte* was so big and they only seemed to hang out with other *Sonido* kids. *Caballo* was notorious for throwing parties, because the R.A. was never there on the weekend. I'd be walking friends home from rehearsal and hear kids shouting and music blaring from the upstairs common room. I was shy and didn't want to walk into the party by myself, so I'd stand outside smoking cigarettes with my fellow music nerds, hoping she'd come out.

Smoke Break

She pulled out a pack of Benson and Hedges from her hoodie pocket, and offered me one.

"Got a light?"

I struck a match and lit her cigarette. "It's okay, I'm not into menthols." A Marlboro Red was already reaching my lips.

"You're not worried about your dad catching you?" I could hear genuine concern in her voice.

"Nah… he started smoking when he was around my age." I tried to convince myself that I didn't care about getting caught. I usually never smoked when my dad was around. I didn't think she would say yes. I thought she'd decline and we'd hang out, waiting for lecture to start. We smoke in silence. I try to read her as she smokes. I see that she's a fast smoker. Benson and Hedges only come in hundred form and she's almost done. I barely am halfway on my Red.

"Looks like it's time to go in…" Most of the smokers have already walked in; others have left altogether. I hesitate, as I say the words. I want to prolong our time together. She drops her cigarette to the ground, and puts it out with her flip-flop. I inhale one last drag, drop my cigarette on the ground as well, and put it out with my shoe.

She moves towards the door and I follow her. I notice her ponytail sway back and forth. "Blink-182" is emblazoned on the back of her hoodie. She must've gotten the hoodie at the welcome week concert. "St. Mark's High School" is screened on the side of her sweatpants. Catholic schoolgirl? She holds the door open for me, and I hesitate to walk through the door. I move to hold it open and let her in. She looks at me confused and again, we're so close, only this time I feel like I should move in for a kiss.

She laughs. "What's going on here?"

I feel the heat rise to my face. "Hah, I don't know…"

She walks into class and waits for me to close the door. We walk to our row and she lets me walk in first, since my chair is further inside the row. We're one of the last two to take our seats. My dad has already begun lecture. I can't pay attention; not that I normally do. I grew up listening to him practice this lecture in his office. The information is familiar; I can finally get credit for it, as a student. I watch Diane diligently take notes.

"It would be helpful if you read before lecture. If anything, before discussion. I'd like to hear you talk. I get tired of my own voice, people." Lecture's over, and I see Diane close her notebook and shift in her seat. The sounds of zippers opening backpacks, papers shuffling, and notebooks closing dominate the room. She gets up and adjusts the straps of her backpack. Is she waiting for me to pack up?

Late Night Adventures

"What hall are you in?"

She *is* waiting for me to pack up!

"Oh, I don't live in the dorms. I'm still at my parents' house." I nod to my dad, below.

"Ahhh. So, whatcha gonna do now? Did you eat yet? This class sucks. It's at dinnertime. I was going to go to C.C., but I didn't have time to eat!" She talks so fast. I hear her questions, but I didn't know anyone could say so many things in one breath.

"C.C.?" I know it stands for *Comida Comuns*, since I've been there before with my friends from *Sonido*. I play dumb, so we can talk a little bit longer.

"Duh, you don't live in *Corte*. *Comida Comuns.* It's like the cafeteria. The food is gross, but it's free. Well not free, since I'm paying for it." I feel myself getting caught up in her world.

"You wanna grab something to eat?" Be cool, Topher. Be cool.

"Sure. What's around here? I don't have a car, so the only thing I know is In-N-Out across the street!" She laughs at her carelessness.

In my head, I run through the list of late night spots that I would go to in high school. Fatburger? Denny's? Lee's? Norms? No In-N-Out, she's already been there.

"Norms?" Hopefully she likes cheap steak and eggs.

She tugs on the end of her hoodie string.

"Sure, why not."

Ch 7: The Story

Room 304

"What are we going to do about *Lolo's* birthday?"

My family has planned a huge birthday bash for my grandfather's ninety-fifth birthday. Dad was supposed to assume his usual role, as family photographer. Mom had helped with the budget for the party. *Lolo* trusted Mom with money because she was just as tight with pennies as he was.

"I'm not going, you have to go." There is no emotion in dad's voice.

"I don't want to go, Pops. Everyone's going to feel sorry for me!"

"Diane, you have to go. Someone from our family has to go. I'm not leaving mom."

I stare at the floor. The flecks in the tiles don't seem to have faded over time. The heart monitor steadily beeps, and I watch as a green line rises and falls. I see *Tita* Nitcole and *Tito* Mitch approach mom's room.

"*Lolo's* party is tonight. You both are going." I fall deeper and deeper into my chair. I sink myself into the seat, believing that it will save me from going to the party.

"Diane's going. I'm staying here." Dad answers for the both of us.

Tita Nitcole's face flinches. "You're going too."

Dad doesn't move. I know he won't move. He pulls out a small reporter's notepad from his jacket pocket. Every hour, he writes down mom's blood pressure. He looks at the past eleven hours' worth of blood pressure readings. In another pocket is a rosary. He prays and prays and prays. Sometimes, I catch his red eyes sliding into sleep. It's never rest, just short naps. *Tita* Nitcole knows this can't last for much longer, or he will get sick.

"I'm going, *Tita*. Dad will stay here with mom. Just in case…"

She doesn't like my reply, but she accepts it. She has to accept it. No one has told my grandfather that one of his children is in the hospital. If I don't go to the party, he will know something is wrong. I think my family doubts my *Lolo's* intelligence.

Happy Birthday, Lolo

I'm one of the last guests to arrive. I feel my relatives' stares as I step into the room. Everyone knows, but him. I take my seat next to my cousin Lee. His goofy laugh relaxes me. I meekly smile, as I try to get comfortable.

"How ya doin'?" It's the question I've been dreading. I feel like everyone's waiting for me to respond. It's supposed to be a celebration, but everyone's walking on eggshells around me.

"Ehh." It's my standard response. It's been my standard response at most family gatherings, but sitting at that table I can't verbalize any other response.

My *Ate* Bee comes by our table. "You okay?"

I appreciate the concern, but I really don't want to deal with it. I look at my watch. All I have to do is get through two hours, and then I can go back to the hospital. I look at the door. "Where is he?"

"Where's who, your dad?" Lee asks me in between crispy wonton noodle bites.

"Nah, dad's with mom. Topher." *Ate* Bee raises her eyebrows, as she eavesdrops on the conversation. "Topher? Your **boyfriend**??"

I answer her with my eyes, "You can take your claws out of me *Ate*. Go pick on someone else tonight." My voice sweetly responds, "No *Ate,* just a friend."

Disappointed with my response, *Ate* Bee moves onto my cousin Eve; her shoulders flinch as *Ate* Bee begins to interrogate her. "Sorry," I silently mouth the word to Eve. "Thanks," she responds back with a long eye-roll. I'm thankful to no longer be in *Ate* Bee's clutches, but truly sorry that she's got her hooks on Eve. The first course arrives, and the waiter begins ladling seafood chowder on several bowls lining the curve of the lazy susan resting in the center of the table.

"Hey you…" Topher slips into a chair next to me.

"Yo." I slurp seafood chowder. Lee nods his head to Topher, as he bites into shrimp he's fished out of his bowl.

Ate Bee sees a new face at our table and, like a vulture, swoops in. "Why hello there, Topher! We've heard so much about you." I laugh at her. She doesn't even try to cover up her snarkiness.

"Oh, really? I've heard so much about you." Topher smiles back. *Ate* Bee giggles a response; he's worked his charm on her. Topher's always had a way with girls. When we're out, girls hover
68

around him. I've tried to play wingman for him, but he never closes the deal. I've never understood why. *Ate* Bee holds her Stepford-wife pose, before heading back to her own table.

"Grrrreat, now she's gonna be hounding me about you for the rest of the night!" I pinch his arm.

"Ow!" He slaps my hand away. "I can't help it if I'm charming." The Cheshire cat-like grin on his face breaks into a familiar laugh.

Sitting with Lee and Topher makes the party a little easier. This isn't any ordinary family party. If it were we wouldn't be sitting in a banquet hall being served mediocre Chinese food. Ordinary family parties take place in a relative's house with a buffet table of potluck food, *Tito* Mitch singing on the Magic Mic, and mom gossiping with the other aunties.

I concentrate on the meal and think to myself, I just might make it through this party. My *Tita* Red comes up to me and whispers in my ear four words I don't want to hear,

"Diane, bless your *Lolo*."

Ch 8: Garden Stories

Spring Break Memories

"Put these away, Diane." *Tita* Red used to get cards with different plants on them, in the mail. The cards were part of a set that lived in its own notebook.

"*Tita,* why do we have these?" It was spring break, and staying with my grandparents and auntie was free daycare.

"They're for *Lolo*, for his garden." *Lolo* Geraldo spent his mornings tending to his garden; grape vines, corn stalks, and strawberry fields lined the backyard.

"What does he do with them?" My nine year old hands unwrap the cellophane surrounding each carefully packaged card.

"*Basiyo* the table, *dai*." From the kitchen, *Lola* Betsy affectionately asks me to set the table.

"OKAY, *Lola!*" I shout from the living room. The cards quickly join the others, in a vinyl notebook titled, "Garden Stories." I don't bother alphabetizing them. The smell of garlic fried rice overpowers me. I run into the kitchen and grab four of everything: plates, forks, and spoons. Placemats left from dinner the night before are still on the table. There is an order to *Lola's* dining table: Plate in the center of the placemat; fork and spoon onto the center of the plate. When I'm finished, I walk into the kitchen and feel the steam from the pot of rice.

"Is this ready?" *Lola* cools *adobo* scooped onto a wooden spoon with her breath, and feeds me. I munch on the fresh dish.

"Mmhmmm," I smile as the chicken adobo melts in my mouth. The soy sauce, vinegar, bay leaves, and brown sugar have marinated to the perfect blend.

"Good?" She laughs at my response. "Go get your *Lolo*."

I scamper to the kitchen door that exits out to the backyard.

"*Lolo! Lolo!* Lunch is ready!" *Lolo* Geraldo inspects his grapevine and brings a colander of freshly picked grapes with him. I meet him in the strawberry patch. "*Lola* made *adobo!*" I excitedly exclaim. He smiles at me, as I tug at his garden-gloved free hand.

Back to the Party

"Happy Birthday, *Lolo*..." The back of his fingers pressed against my forehead. He smiles at me, like he did back then. *Lolo* Geraldo pulls me to the seat next to him, before I can let go and head back to my seat.

"Diane, *saan sa mommy mo?*" He knows. *Tita* Red tries to save me. "Papa..." He stops her with a stare. It's been a week and my relatives still haven't told him. They're waiting for the right time. I think they underestimate *Lolo's* intelligence.

"She's sick."

I will not participate in my family's cover up.

Lolo's eyes meet mine. "I knew something was going on..."

Return to Spring Break Memories

"Diane, will you please say grace?" Being the youngest means you get told what to do, a lot.

"Yes *Lola.*" *Lolo, Lola, Tita* Red, and I make the sign of the cross. I speed through the prayer as fast as I can. "Bless us, oh Lord. And these thy gifts. Which we are about to receive. From thy bounty through Christ. Our Lord. Amen."

When I'm done, *Lola* laughs and begins to spoon a chicken leg onto my plate, while *Tita* Red serves me a small mountain of rice. A fork and spoon are ready in my hands. The phone rings. "Can I answer it?" I look to my aunt. She nods her head yes, and I run to the phone.

"Hello?" My parents had just started letting me answer the phone.

"Diane? It's your mom, where's *Lola?*" She usually calls around lunch to check up on me, make sure I'm not acting up.

"We're eating lunch. *Lola* made chicken *adobo*. We just started. *LOLAAA!* Mom wants to talk to you!" I talk at rapid speed, and with no volume control. *Lola* takes the phone from my hand, and I make a mad dash back to my place at the table. Lunch is getting cold. *Lola* tells mom I've slept most of the morning away. I get dropped off at their house so early in the morning, I still have my pajamas on. When I come in, I snuggle into the couch and wrap myself up in the blankets used as couch coverings. The sound of *Lola's* ABC soap operas, and the smell of lunch being prepared, wakes

71

me from my slumber. *Tita* Red comes home from working the graveyard shift at the post office, and I help her around the house. I find ways to amuse myself by running around the backyard, and playing in *Lolo's* garden.

"Diane, can you help me in the garden today?" *Lolo* perfectly cuts his chicken with a fork and spoon. He never uses his hands to eat. In the Philippines, he was a bigwig with former Philippine president, Carlos Garcia. They were both *Boholanos,* and when Garcia was in office *Lolo* Geraldo became a big time auditor. Sometimes, when *Lolo* is out in his garden, I rummage through old photos of him and *Lola* in the Philippines. They look so glamorous in these vintage black and white photographs. *Lolo* Geraldo looks strong and confident in a simple *barong tagalog,* while *Lola* Betsy looks graceful and beautiful in a *piña* dress that fits her slim body. *Lolo* and *Lola* were guests at several presidential dinners. This is where *Lolo* perfected his eating habits. He was such an expert at eating with a fork and spoon he could remove the skin off a shrimp without using his hands.

"Uh huh." I would never perfect that skill. I was too much like *Lola* Betsy. *Lola* loved to eat with her hands. I learned how to skillfully spoon rice and chicken, with my fingers. "What do you want me to help you with, *Lolo?*"

Time for Cake

"Let's cut the cake!" *Tita* Red tries to change the subject.

"What do you want me to help you with, *Lolo?*" I look into his eyes and see myself in his glasses. Why can't I be nine years old again, helping him in his garden?

He pats my hand, and it calms me. *Lolo* has changed in the past ten years. When we lost *Lola* Betsy, everything in the family changed. We lost our heart. *Lolo* lost his spark. But when *Ate* Bee had Chloe, he began to come around. Seeing his great-grandchild running around made him happy again. I didn't want mom's sickness to make him sad again.

"Take me to your mom."

Ch 9: Driving Stories

It feels strange having *Lolo* in the passenger seat. When I drive, I feel invincible. I weave through cars at a rapid pace. With *Lolo* by my side, I hesitate to merge. I find myself slowly inching behind a car, driving at the 35mph speed limit.

"*Sus! Bagal naman...*" I hear him whisper under his breath. He's just like mom; while dad would drive, she would complain, "Jesus, they drive so slow!"

I change lanes and speed up. He's in a hurry to see her. I no longer feel that rush. I sometimes drive slow, on purpose. The longer it takes to get to my destination, the more I believe she'll be better by the time I get there.

"Remember when you were little and we would watch all you kids playing in the front yard?" *Lolo* pats my hand as it rests on the gear shift.

I laugh. "Yeah, I think Lee used to cheat when we played Pepsi/7up!"

A large grin emerges from Lolo's face. "He did."

Pepsi / 7up

"*Eeny, meeny, miny, moe. Catch a tiger by the toe. If he hollers let him go. My mother said. To pick the very best one. And you are not it. YOU'RE IT!*" Lee laughs as he points at me. I stick my tongue out at him and walk to the other end of the yard. Being "it" means you get to shout "Pepsi" or "7up," but it also means you have to chase someone before they reach "home," which is *Tita* Red's beat up yellow Camaro that has never left the driveway.

The game is simple. Whoever is "it" yells "Pepsi" with their back to everyone, and then everyone gets to move forward. To make them stop you turn around, and yell, "7up." The goal is for the other players to tag whoever is "it," first. Then everyone must race back to "home," while the "it" person tags as many people as possible. The people tagged become a part of "it's" team.

Lee always cheats. He never gets chosen as "it," because he's always the one deciding who's it. His strategy is to put his little brother Chuck in front of him. Chuck doesn't know what's going on, as he is usually wrapped up in whatever lollipop he has that day. Sugar stains constantly line his cheeks. When I try to tag Lee, Chuck always ends up tackling me with his sticky fingers. I don't mind it; we form a team afterwards. Team, "Beat Lee!"

When Lee lost Chuck as his shield, he would pick another younger relative to block for him. He would do this until he was the last kid standing. There would be me, Chuck and Chuck's youngest brother Victor, our older cousins Evan and Alex, all of us, versus Lee. He would outrun us all, to "home." This eventually became his strategy in high school football. It's the reason Lee became All-City Running Back his senior year of high school.

Lee also would creep up before I yelled, "Pepsi." I could never tell, because I had my back to everyone. And everyone else was too wrapped in their own strategy to survive to see Lee inching his way towards tagging me.

We would play before dinner, and *Lolo* would watch us build up an appetite with several games of Pepsi/7up. He would lean against the wood porch railing and laugh at his grandchildren playing in his front yard. Twilight gave way to evening, and hunger would take over our bellies. Being the oldest, Evan or Alex would end the game.

"Who's hungry?" Evan would tickle me, before picking me up from the ground.

"I think *Lola* made fried chicken!" Alex picked up Victor from the grass. Being the youngest at 3, Victor would lose interest in the game and end up sitting in the grass, creating a game of his own. Victor's face lit up at the prospect of fried chicken.

"CHIKN RICE!" he shouts in glee. *Lola's* fried chicken and rice was Victor's favorite meal.

Lee would already be at the porch, rehashing his wins to *Lolo*. "Did you see me *Lolo?!* I beat them all… AGAIN and AGAIN!" He would laugh as he placed the back of *Lolo's* hand to his forehead.

"Bless *Lolo*, Victor." As a toddler, he didn't understand what "bless" was, so Lee would hold *Lolo's* hand and place it on his brother's forehead. Before we entered the house we all would "bless" *Lolo* Geraldo. None of us could imagine a time where we wouldn't have to "bless" him.

KP Woodland Hills

I pull into the parking lot, warm from the happy memory of playing Pepsi/7up with my cousins; the car idles in a spot close the hospital entrance. *Lolo* watches me procrastinate by fiddling with the radio and making sure I have everything in my purse. The gear moves to "Park," and I take the key out of the ignition. A fall breeze whizzes by me as I open my door. *Lolo* walks over to my side of the car, and straightens his jacket.

"Did you bring your dad food?" he asks me while staring at a familiar site. "Uh huh…" I lift the white plastic bag filled with tupperware *baon Tita* Nitcole made for me and dad.

"Okay… let's go." He continues to stare up at the hospital. The fall breeze whizzes through the tufts of what white hair he has left. I take in a deep breath and wait for *Lolo* to take a step. He hesitates.

"*Lolo* Geraldo?"

Ch 10: Smoke Breaks

Lolo Geraldo reaches into his jacket pocket. His hands fish for his rosary.

"*Lolo?* Are you okay?" I wait for him to answer me. My relatives are upset with me for telling him the truth. They didn't want him to know his daughter was in the hospital. *Tita* Nitcole was especially worried that *Lolo* Geraldo would have another heart attack with the news. *Lolo's* stronger than they think. *Tita* Red has put him on a strict diet of fish, vegetables, and rice. He no longer consumes lunches of cholesterol ridden meals like *lechon kiwali* and *kare kare*.

"I wanted to make sure I had my rosary." He pulls out a 3 x 3 plastic envelope that holds his rosary. The scent of rose petals fills the air and I immediately think of *Lola* Betsy.

"I wish *Lola* was here…" My shoulders become heavy with the statement.

"Come on, let's go." *Lolo* moves toward the building. I don't need to show him where to go. He's all too familiar with this routine. He made this trip numerous times for his own wife, and now his daughter.

Pops and Lolo

"We brought you food, Pops." I started calling dad "Pops" again. Before mom got sick, she would address him as *Pops*. It made him smile when I said it. It feels like an American version the *Bisaya* traditional *Papa.*

He gets up from his chair and blesses *Lolo* Geraldo. The practice isn't relegated to his grandchildren; his children and their spouses all pay their respects to the patriarch of the Delgado clan.

Lolo pulls up a chair to mom's bed. He holds her hand and pulls out a St. Jude medallion. He says a prayer and then pins it to mom's hospital gown.

"Make sure she doesn't lose this. When Bet-Bet was here I had to keep replacing it." I nod my head in reply. Dad gets up from his chair.

"Papa, can you stay here with Bing? I'm going to eat outside." I think this is the first time dad's left mom's side all day.

"Is that all you brought?!" *Tita* Nitcole's high pitched voice rings in my ear. "Here, eat this too!" She hands dad more tupperware containers. "Don't eat here. Let's go down to the cafeteria." I know this is her way of getting dad off this floor.

"It's okay. Go eat. You should eat. I'll stay here with Bing." *Lolo's* calming voice reassures us.

I meander about the room. I don't know where to go. I'm not hungry and the food we brought is for dad. Plus, it feels like *Tita* Nitcole and dad want to talk… alone.

"In the name of the father, the son, and the holy ghost." The beads on *Lolo's* rosary click together as he begins to pray. I take the chair on the other side of mom's bed. "I believe in God, the father almighty, creator of heaven and earth…" I can't bring myself to pray out loud.

Why Bother

My relatives have started having weekly prayer meetings, on mom's behalf. Prayer and Jesus have always been a big deal to the Delgados. The last time we prayed like this was after *Lola's* accident. I can't bring myself to pray with them. I'm mad.

God didn't have to do this to her. God didn't have to make her suffer. God didn't have to make us suffer. God didn't have to make *me* suffer.

All the "Our Father's, Hail Mary's, and Glory Be's" in the world aren't bringing me relief. *Lolo* Geraldo, dad, and my aunties and uncles have all found ways to find some relief through prayer.

Smoke Breaks

Instead, I find relief in Benson and Hedges. My knee begins to twitch as *Lolo* announces the second Sorrowful Mystery, "The Scourging in the Pillar." I walk out of the room, tense and frustrated. I don't have the patience for the elevator, so I maneuver my way through the hallways to the exit staircase. The fluorescent lights mark my way out to fresh air that will soon be tainted with tobacco smoke.

I hurriedly take a cigarette out and place it in between my lips. As I fish for my lighter in my pockets, I hear a familiar voice.

"Need a light?"

I inhale and slowly smile. "Thanks… what are you doing here?"

Topher shrugs. "I didn't want to drive all the way back to Irvine with food coma, so I hung out with Lee for a bit. He suggested we come here and visit you."

I peak around for my cousin.

"He went inside. Had to piss." Topher exhales on his Marlboro Red, and explains matter-of-factly.

"Ahh." It's no surprise. Lee has a small bladder. We can never go anywhere without him having to hunt for a bathroom. I told him to get his prostate checked, but he won't listen to me. You think he'd be more mindful of his health, his mom being a nurse and all.

I step away from the doorway as hospital employees begin to bump into me, trying to catch smoke breaks themselves. We head to a concrete bench near an ashtray populated with a cigarette butt forest. We smoke in silence, our shoulders gently tapping against each other. I shiver; the chilly air causes the hairs on my arm to rise. I've left my jacket in mom's room. Topher slides the zipper off his hoodie and places it on my shoulders. I slip my arms into the sleeves.

"Thanks... I left my jacket upstairs. It gets so warm in there."

"Don't worry about it. Here, you still look cold." He scoots in closer to me and wraps his arm around my shoulder. My head seems to rest perfectly in the creak of his shoulder. We finish our cigarettes and toss them onto the sidewalk. Neither one of us moves from the warm embrace.

"I should head in." My nose brushes his neck, and I can see blood rush to Topher's face. "Are you blu..."

His lips meet mine.

My eyebrows crinkle.

His arms bring me in closer.

I fall deeper and deeper into this kiss. Neither one of us want to break away first.

Are we *kissing*? Are we *really kissing*?

Sirens blare as an ambulance drives past. The loud sound startles me and brings me back.

"We should head in..."

Ch 11: He Said. She Said.

Did That Really Happen? Topher's Side

What is she thinking? Damn it! I've got the worst timing ever. Like she really needs this right now. It just felt like the right thing to do. Did she break away first? Is she mad at me? What do I say? Do I tell her how I feel? She's finally got to know how I feel about her now. Right? Right?!

Did That Really Happen? Diane's Side

…

What's going on?

…

There's no denying I didn't like the kiss between me and Topher. But I don't get it. What does this mean? He's never liked me. Well of course he likes me, but he's never *like liked* me. I'm not like the other girls who drool over him at school. Is that why he likes me? So wait… does he like me?

The Elevator

The walk from the concrete bench to the hospital elevator should only take a minute, a minute and a half max. It feels like it's taken us half an hour to get to the elevator. Neither of us pay attention to the elevator as we get in and I hit "3."

"I'm heading to the basement." A man in a lab coat attempts to hit the open button, but we're already moving.

"No worries, we'll just go for a little ride," I hear myself reply.

Just Friends

I've never felt uncomfortable with Topher before. He's my best friend. Sure, I thought he was cute when we first met and I had a mini-crush on him freshman year, but I never thought he reciprocated those feelings.

We've always been *just friends*. He's dated sorority girls, music geeks, and activist chicks. I had my thing with Rich. I never really thought it was a relationship, just a *thing*. We'd hang out after work, hot box in Rich's car, talk shit about our fellow Border's coworkers, and then drive off to his apartment to smoke out some more, play video games, fuck, or do all of the above. I never went into the details with Topher. I tried to once, and he got all weird. He never liked Rich and when we tried hanging out together, Topher was a jerk. I guess you could say Topher got jealous.

Rich vs. Topher

"Why do you hang out with that guy?" There's an extra-irritated tone in Topher's voice. He must've just broken up with Cindy. Or was it Carli. I can never keep up.

"I dunno. He's funny. Rich makes work go by faster. And he's always got herb." I don't have any real feelings for Rich. We were work friends, who just so happen to like the same video games. One night we were both playing *Goldeneye,* and I was losing as usual...

Rich

"You just blew yourself up with a mine." Rich laughs as my character dies.

"I suck," I lament my obvious suckiness.

"Yeah, you do." He snickers at me and I try to punch him in the arm. Tragically, I miss and Rich grabs my wrist and pulls me into his lap.

"What are you trying to do?" The giggles hit me.

"Well, first I'm going to end this game by killing your man for the millionth time." With a flick of his wrist on the Nintendo 64 controller, the game is over and I'm dead, yet again. "And then I'm going to do this." He leans in, I drop my controller, and we find ourselves in a passionate, marijuana induced embrace.

"I think I'm better at this," I whisper as I maneuver through FHM and Stuff magazines to his room.

Topher's Opinion

"Eww. T.M.I. T.M.I. Too much info, Diane." His face is pale.

"Fine. Fine." I always cut him off before he tells me about his latest fling. "Why don't you like Rich?"

"I dunno... I just think you could do better." He shrugs as we enter lecture. We're late, so we find two seats in the back row and the conversation never resumes.

The *thing* between Rich and me ended when he got a girlfriend and I gave up smoking herb. Besides video games, smoking out, and sleeping with each other, there wasn't much we could really talk about. I quit working at the store and got a better paying office job closer to school. I dated a few guys here and there, but to be honest Topher ruined my game. We hung out so often, that I got the impression everyone at school thought we were together. Even Noel and Will had their suspicions about the two of us.

Secret Lovers

"Come on... you and Topher? There's nothing going on?" Will pesters me as he bites into a slice of pizza.

"Dude. Ga-ross. How could you say that?! We're like brother and sister!" I use a napkin to soak up the oil of my slice.

"It must be some *Flowers in the Attic* type shit." Noel's already downed his soda and is getting up for a refill.

"Shut the fuck up, Noel. That's sick." My napkin is orange from the grease. "Ugh, that's gross, but this is delicious." I fold my slice and devour the cheesy goodness.

"Diane, everyone thinks the two of you are together. And if you aren't hittin' that, there's something wrong with you. You know there are girls in class who are ready to swoop in on Topher." Will's already moved on to his second slice.

"Well... where are the guys ready to swoop in on me?" I take a long sip of my soda. Damn, I should've had Noel refill my drink too.

"Dude, you're a dude. That's why no one's gonna swoop in on you." Noel tries to take his seat, but I kick the chair away from him. "*See?*"

"You're an asshole, Noel." I retort.

"Yes I am, as are you." He smirks back.

"I know." We all laugh together. This is why we're friends. We're all such jerks to each other. I think that's the reason why I can't get find a decent guy. I hang out with assholes all day long.

Elevator Go Up

The elevator doesn't even have the decency to have lame elevator music. I can sense both of us feel weird. Topher doesn't have a snarky comeback; neither do I. I tug at the zipper of his hoodie. It smells like Marlboro Reds.

Am I ready for this?

My eyes are weary from days of crying about mom. My body is tired from school, work, and trips back home. I need something.

I reach for Topher's hand.

"Diane?" I squeeze his palm. It's the only answer I can give.

The elevator doors open. Lee's waiting for the two of us. My shoulder bumps Topher's arm as we step out of the elevator. I breathe a sigh of relief and start to chuckle. Lee's eyes dart straight for our hands holding each other.

"What the hell?! I just went to the bathroom!"

Ch 12: Letters in the Wind

Dear God,

Things have been pretty rough lately. I don't understand why you are doing this. I don't understand why all these things are happening. If I quit smoking, will you make mom better? If I finish school, will you make mom better? If I come home every weekend and stay by her side, will you make mom better?

You have very odd timing. Why do I have feelings for my best friend now? After all these years? Do I really need to deal with all this love stuff now? I can barely think straight and you send one more thing at me. Is there a bullseye on my forehead?

Can you send me an answer?

Me

Dear Lola Betsy,

Sitting on your grave site gives me solace. Can you hear me as I write these words? It's been six years since you've left us, but I still miss you. Please don't take mom away.

Love,

Me

Dear Pops,

Tita Nitcole told me you're getting sick. I'm not supposed to know, but I do. You have to eat real food. Your caloric intake cannot only be Chivas Regal every night. I can't lose you too.

I'm scared,

Me

Dear Topher,

We have to talk.

Call me later,

Me

Ch 13: Postcards in Dreams

Memories in Night Time Reveries

Lola Betsy answered my letter in a dream. More a memory of her in a dream.

It's winter break, and I'm going to Stoney Crest elementary school. Mom couldn't leave me at home alone, and we didn't have household help like the rich kids at Stoney Crest. Instead, I would always go to *Lola* Betsy's house.

In this memory I'm sick yet again; my weak immune system makes me a sick kid, growing up. I enter the house with my blankets and baby pillow in tow as I crawl onto the itchy, from the 70s, couch and try to get comfortable. *Lola* Betsy makes me "chocolate *lugow*," something she always made for her own children when they were sick.

Chocolate *lugow* is basically *champarado,* or chocolate rice porridge. But growing up, this is what I called it. Even though I'm sniffling and I can't breathe, my *Lola's* "chocolate *lugow*" always makes me feel better. The steam from the bowl cures me for the time I'm eating. I can breathe and smile again. She watches me eat and makes sure I'm alright, before cleaning up the dishes and pot she used to make the dish .

Lola asks, "Do you want some more?"

I eagerly shake my snot-ridden face, "Yes!" as she pours the last spoonsful into my bowl. My small hands grab my spoon and dive into my second serving and I, for that short while, forget I'm sick.

Lola Betsy is my protector in the ten hours that I stay with her, while my mom and dad are at work. She lets me sleep on her couch as she watches her soap operas, and I follow along with her stories as I drift in and out consciousness. The comfort of her home is all a sick kid like me needs. I'm sick, happy, content, and loved all at once.

Unconditional love

I wake up and feel *Lola* Betsy in the room. I almost expect her to be there in the room and have a conversation with her, like I did with *Lola* Ling. The room is empty, but I don't feel it. Tears swim on my cheeks as I think about the memory. This memory taught me unconditional love, because *Lola* was unconditional love.

I ask her not to take mom away, and as I wipe away the tears
and drift back to sleep,
I know she won't.

GRACE YOUNG

Dear Dorothy: July 11, 2008

It has been too long since we have last corresponded. So instead of counting up, this is the final countdown!! Thirty-five more days until you are in my arms. Thirty-five more days until we are once again united.

It's hard being away from someone you have never, minus that brief tragix (YES!) year in high school, not spoken to in twenty-four hours. I guess that we speak every twenty-four hours, but the time difference between Hong Kong and Home make the space and time continuum static and disconnect.

Today was frustrating. I feel like our house is a crazy place, everyone is always talking all at once. Rarely listening. Playing weird music that sounds like the China-ese national anthem. Since you are so close to the mainland, please let me know if being closer to there changes your emotions about China. I think I am too nationalistic about Taiwan, or that everyone I meet from Taiwan is a specific kind of crazy that is like our mom. They are funny, laugh too much, eat too much, pray too much, and are easily excited by way to nice things. I have been frustrated because people from China stay at our house and wake me when I assume it is day there, but the day has not begun for me! It's been loud. Then, at night, my mom and dad urge me into my room of solitude and silence (I am not 2 tragix!), because I whisper on the phone. Okay. Except last night I was not whispering.

I am glad that my sadness stopped me from being a sulking weeper and got me to go online in the dark of the night (she was tossing and turning) to e-stalk el boyfriend Steven Ma. I really do love him. I really do. I am just really scared. I am uncomfortable knowing that I am dependent on him just the tiniest bit. I don't like how upset I get when he says he is busy, but everyone knows I am just too selfish.

Speaking of selfish. I am not selfish to name this after me!!! I have always desired– longed– PINED for something named after me but alas, there is always some forty-one year old woman from Florida who wants to fall in love and get a tan who has been selfish before me. I wish the best for her. I do. Mainly because I love her myspace picture because it was washed out and sultry. Sultry is in!

I think I write too sporadic. I think I tangent (thought humorous, it is not clear!!!!). Actually, today my mom pulled me aside, and gave me *gua zi* (watermelon seeds 100% made in Taiwan) so I would listen to her. She basically told me that my hysteria last night (it was not hysteria, more like a lot of late night talking while she sat downstairs working) was because I am not a clear communicator. I was like "Srsly. Wtf. You don't even know me. BITCHES GET SHIT DONE!!!" No. Okay. Mostly the first two sentences. One word makes a sentence, sometimes. Also that is a complaint of Sma's. When he isn't praising me and telling me how it will kill me and assume everything about me so that he can name things GraceYOUNG! No. Okay. Mostly the first thing. Anyways. I am looking at what these different writers create, and yes. I should outline. That's how you score so well on essays. Also, that is how I score.

HAHA. APPARENTLY NOT ACCORDING TO MY MOTHER.

Forever and non-endingly yours because your blood is my blood and your mother fed you and me from her body even though that is pretty nasty to think about I also watched the trailer for Orgasmic Birth and basically never want to give birth no matter how natural it is and the amazing organism it will give me because orgasms are a few minutes... A BABY IS A LIFETIME!!

- Grace Young

Hay Dorothy Young: July 11, 2008

I'm waking up much later than I normally do. I woke up at 10:30 today!! I need to wake up around around 7:30!! I need to be successful!!

So I wake up, eat breakfast, and then check my mail because of the letters that mom wants us to write. Guess what I found out!! Your driving fail has caused our shitty insurance company to drop us!! Haha. It's okay though, Mom got all srs bidnezz on the Ellen lady because I guess this is the second time this summer when they failed to contact us to let us know. Mom is annoyed and said she is sorry is being a "BITCH." I love it when mom uses those words. She is so vulgar!!!

Last night good friend Jake and I went to get free Slurpees from 7-11, and they did not give them to us. How can something be broadcasted nationally, nay, GLOBALLY if it is not true. Let us review the facts:

1) Facebook Group - A trustworthy source. I was reading *the Extras* by Scott Westerfield (HUZZAH YOUNG ADULT SCIENCE FICTION!) and they talk about something called the power of the crowd. Someone somewhere is bound to know something about anything, so if over four hundred thousand people say there will be free Slurpees, there MUST be free Slurpees.

(Side note now: Mom just said that we should change our insurance person to the big guy. I was like, the racist one? But he is Spanish!!! Mom, he is still a racist.)

2) Slurpee.com - the Slurpee website that is linked from the official 7-11 website. They say at participating locations. But when you click on the find locations link, they deceive you by plotting all the 7-11's in your vicinity. Note: There are seven in a five mile radius around our home. All within biking distance, huzzah!

Okay, those are my only two points. I am supposed to go pick up Jake to search for more Slurpees, but Mom wants me to write about things for her. I can't do it. My brain is wornnnnn ouutttttttt.

- Grace "plz gv m brn frz frm ck slrpz plz" Young

UGHHHHHOROTHY!: July 14, 2008

I am so so tired. It was muggy today, and way too warm. Why is it humid in LA?! I think the smog is a blanket that steams us open. It sounds like a good idea for your pores, but the dirty air just fills them with crap and you get pimples. Luckily, only my forehead (hidden by my bounty of bangs) has been mildly cursed. Thank Mom for USANA. Seriously.

I washed my car, too. It's so tiring to wash cars with no soap. I am using this awesome microfiber cloth I guess Mom bought years ago. And she made a trip to the 99cent store and got a new squeegee. It sucks compared to that hardcore black one that broke (I think). But on the plus side, it is all primary colors. On the negative side, it kind of sucks.

Steven Ma came by today for a bit. I was feeling not here. I just want to sit around. Seriously. Also I drew for like, two hours. It will be framed and go above your bed or something. Mega intricate. Then we (minus Sma) went to eat at this restaurant called "Indian." It's in the plaza where Uncle Joes Donuts is. If you can ignore the disrespect to Native Americans, it's a fucking cool place. It's really really really good Taiwanese food (and you know me and Mom are sharks about that), and the decor is really cool. The servers are all these hot Taiwanese girls wearing denim short shorts and orange shirt (Hooters?) with really fab hair. Also, the people who own it are Taiwanese people who go to EFC Arcadia. It's neat. We will bike there. Wait… San Gabriel Blvd's streets are shit. All crumbly and full of crazy Mom drivers. Woot.

Something to think about: By time you are back, Grom won't be a pastor any more.

Last night I dreamt I was the captain of a boat and I had to feed the crew (because I'm a woman. NOT!! It's my ship!!!!!!) and all the food was in those pop top cans. All the tabs kept falling off and I couldn't figure out how to open them… Even though in real life I know how. Other stuff happened, but I don't remember.

UGHHHH. Tired. I'll write about yesterday tomorrow… Hmmmmmmmm.

- Grace "Mosquitoes Only Bite One Side of My Body" Young

DOROT OO KEWL FOR SKEWL: July 20, 2008

I totally forgot a day. UGHHHHH. Failure!!! Sadness. Remorse. Utter and complete JOY TO THE WORLD!

Today was devastatingly boring and wonderful. I woke up, ate breakfast (with my good friends Harry and Hermoine, because Ron was all lyke "YOU DON'T KNOW WUT CHOR DOIN ARRY!!" and I was like "Nooo THANKS RON!"), and then Dad came home and demanded that I bathe. So I did and then we went to In-n-Out where I was confronted by all the great faces from high school (it was the best!! NOT!!!!) and then we went to Ross, and then TJ Maxxxxx to try and find me black dress pants, to no avail. But, on a side note, one amazing discovery is that TJ Maxxxxxx has Micheal Kors and THEORY! It is super fabulous and there is this beautiful Theory coat in navy blue that I would wear if I could spend my life being fabulous and walking the streets (not street walking tsk tsk) with a baguette and traveling from one *niu rou mien* store to the next eating all the delightful beef noodles soups scrumpdiliumpcious! Only one thing fit me supremely and it was this Theory shirt but it costed like, seventy bucks and I was like no thanks Dad even though he is way mega generous. Then we came home, got Gma and Zhang Ahhhh yeeee and then we dropped her off and went to the mall. Dad made me look in JC Penny but I was like NO THNX and went to H&M and spent a lot of time trying on a bunch of black pants and now have a decently fine pair and a long sleeve light blue shirt. All for fifty five bucks. THNX to H&M for not being all fabulous like Theory, though that shirt was too fab for me! (Srsly).

Okay, I am drawing up a storm surprise for you and that is all you get. Also, yesterday me and my small friend Mandy Sui took a shit load of Cue photos.

Srsly. Only children people. Some I like, and others I rly h8. Mandy Sui is so sweet because she is one that I think really really really wanted more siblings but her parents were like hmm NO THNX! She was really excited when I went to her house and she was jumping around and it was cute because she pretty much comes up to my armpits. Smells gr8. OK! My point is you and me are too much of good ambassadors of fabulousity.

Sma is at a wedding today and he looks so fab. Also, your BF Davide Morihiro called me this morning and was all lyke, do you want a Members Only Jacket because he found a fakkkkkkke one in dark

91

purple but I was like NO THNX I have one like that. If you can, find me one in black so me and Sma and you can match forever and make a gang. Except not all that. I will tell him that later.

To spare from all this consumerist bull shit: My lips are all puffy from too much sun and maybe someone poisoned my chapstick.

SO MOM NEWS: (highlight of everything). Mom calls me yesterday and is like, "DIANA AHHH YEE HAS A FRIEND FROM THE EAST" (to which I replied New York or China?) and my mom was all like "NEW YORKKKKK. OKAY SO CAN YOU DRIVE HER BACK TO IRVINE. AND TOMORROW TAKE HER TO UCLA AND THEN DRIVE HER BACK AND THEN DRIVE HER WITH YOU TO IRVINE ON SUNDAY, WHEN YOU GO BACK??!?!?!" and I was all like. Okay. But Sma won't be at UCLA so she was like, okay okay okay. And then today went to UCLA with this random person (too nice I hope she demanded gas money) because she was this person to do USANA. UGHHHHH.

KAY! TTY ON GCHAT!

-GRACE YOUNG
AHHHHHHHHHHHHHHHHHHHHHHHHHHHHHHHHH

My Darling Sister: July 24, 2008

It has been farrrrrrr too long since I have last corresponded with thee. I pray that the weather in Hong Kong is well, though it is a foreign land. Mine computer in the office doth not have spell check, thoughst I rarely check those things. They challenge thinge perfection that tis mine English.

I have begun to run on the elliptical in the morning at 7:30 so I can get to work pronto. There is this nice old lady who is there too. She likes to watch the Today Show. I lost my earphones so I am using this pair that I found in my desk. Only one ear side works. So the Today Show it is.

Yesterday I hung out with Melissa Chan. It was fun. I went to Forever 21 (bleh!!!!! but their underwear fits my disproportional [though absolutely perfect because low self esteem is soo six years ago] body) and found the lumberjack underwear!!!! I got a purple pair and another pair of red ones and a black pair to be safe. It's the best!!!

Since my boss told us that we could wear whatever we want, I am totally wearing my gray Cheap Mondays and my man brogue shoes and a black tank and my grey motorcycle jacket (different shades of gray/grey!!!) and I feel tres nineteen nineties (Dude WTF HOW DO YOU SPELL THOSE WERDS!) and I am really really feeling it.

I talked things out with Kevin and it makes more sense. He didn't cancel our plans to go on a date with a *baii ren*, but rather he canceled our plans to meet with the marketing people for RAGE! LOL!!!!!! SRSLY!!!! I am so excited he is going to be the next flier boiiii. LOLLLLLLLLLLL. Call the conductor because the party train is out of CONTROL!!!!! WORK IT GIRL! You crazy Michael Jackson thizzmaster.

I am kind of sad that you are doing that stuff without me but I know that it your loss because I will walk it out like no other. It's on. I have my game face fa sho.

I've been drawing a lot. I'm kind of excited. I also like elderly folk. They know more than we will ever know! I am going to be BUCA DE BEBOOOO (how do you spell that. DAMN this no spell check!!! DAMN IT!) on Friday for Kevin's B-Day. I'm excited because I will eat my weight in sphagetti (that doesn't look spelled right either... =C) because I love that stuff mondo much.

93

{ who the hell do we think we are }

PEACE!
-Grace "Big Spender" Young

PS: I have to print the entire website under construction (I used about two inches of paper yesterday and that is around half the website) and then cut and taped it together to be cohesive. Seriously. Also, I have to database 95 stuff. I've done like... 69... LOL!. RAGE FTW!

PSS: It's super chill. I'm going to get water now. NO COMPLAINTS PLZ.

ERIK MATSUNAGA

Land of Enchantment

Pete's uncle Al sat shotgun. It was midnight plus thirty as they cruised through a starry strip of New Mexico desert highway. Al had accompanied Pete on this cross-country drive, by way of Chicago to Los Angeles, for lack of anything better to do.

"You still okay?" Al asked. In eighteen hours, Pete had not surrendered the wheel. "You want me to drive?"

"Nah."

"Shit man," said Al. "I'm the one who should be tired. I'm old. Man, I'm fifty-five years old, you know how old that is?"

Pete's eyes were glued to the tail lights of a semi.

"Eh, it's not that old."

"You got no fucking clue how old that is," Al said. "Fifty-five years is a long time to be alive, man. How long does a fly get, a week? Dogs get what, ten? Fifteen years? I've been on this planet for fifty-five fucking years, man. That's a long time."

The semi exited a rest stop, and Pete pressed the gas in search of another to draft.

"Yeah, I guesso."

"Funny thing is," Al continued, "I made it this far, through all this shit - war and women, a ninth grade education, and now at the end of it all, I play it safe. Wear a seatbelt. Smoke filtered, light cigarettes. Drink light beer. Diet pop. Chew sugarless gum. Fuck with a condom. How fuckin' backwards is that, man?"

"Pretty fuckin' backwards, man."

There were no trucks ahead; Pete's eyelids began to droop.

"Lemme tell you something, man," Al said. "I never gave you any uncle type advice, but don't listen to everyone who spouts on about how short life is. You have no fucking clue how long it can be."

"Sometimes."

"You got pretty good genes; unless you get shot or hit by a car you got another what, fifty, sixty years in you? You have no idea all the shit's coming your way. Haha, I feel sorry for you, man."

Al cracked his window and lit a cigarette.

"You never know," Pete replied. "I could get shot or hit by a car. Maybe fall asleep at the wheel."

"You okay? You want me to drive? I'm wide awake, man."

"Alright."

Pete pulled off on a dark ramp to nowhere, got out, pissed on the road, slid into the passenger seat, and knocked out until Flagstaff.

{ who the hell do we think we are }

Obsoletion

```
<html>
<head>
<title>obsoletion</title>
</head>
<body bgcolor="#ffffff">
<br>
<font face="arial,helvetica" size="2" color="#333333">
nobody uses static html<br>
anymore.<br><br>
guess it's like using<br>
an abacus;<br><br>
though i'd rather know<br>
an abacus<br>
over a calculator.<br><br>
what if you run out<br>
of batteries?
</font>
</body>
</html>
```

Commitment

da Barber said he wanted a nice healthy steak, so he could feel like a million bucks.

"Enough a dis no eatin' meat on Fridays; I did it my whole life! I gotta have sometin' healty, ya know what I mean? A big steak wid'all da protein I need all day; make me feel like a million bucks! I should do dat, ya know? Cook one up, and uhhh, yeah I'm too old ta be feelin' like shit cuz I ain't eatin' right! Ey, uhh, I done'nis my whole life, ya hear what I'm tellin' ya? I deserve a good meal on Fridays; I work my ass off all week, ya know what I mean? And I ain't goin'ta Hell for it!"

da Barber got up and disappeared to the kitchen, returning with three hardboiled eggs, a block of sharp cheddar, and a jar of horseradish.

{ who the hell do we think we are }

a dream

i could see her only
from the shoulders down.

halter top and me,
in a midevening room.

she spun a box
atop a coffee table.

"let's play backgammon," she said.

"i don't know how," i said.

Westside Eulogy

The bungalow's French doors were just wide enough for the Datsun to fit through. The car rolled slowly into the front room, where Teddy Atsumori sat watching television. Teddy Atsumori, in a panic, flipped over the back of the couch. The Datsun tractorly pushed the couch into the lath and plaster wall, squashing Teddy Atsumori like a fly.

Driving up Centinela Avenue, Ike Sekidera casually asked Ebb Eguchi if he wanted a hamburger. Ebb was in a daze. When Ike's 280z rolled up his driveway earlier that afternoon, a hamburger was all Ebb had expected for the day; Ike had stopped by to see if Ebb wanted to grab a quick bite. Now, Ebb was witness to a murder. But, he kept this to himself.

"Hamburger sounds good," Ebb said.

Ike pulled the 280z into the lot of Mago's Famous Hamburgers. They walked in; Ike ordered a *teriyaki* avocado burger with a Coke, and Ebb got a *chashu* avocado burrito with a strawberry milkshake. Ike paid, despite Ebb's every effort.

Ebb bit into the burrito, thinking on how the mix of mashed, barbecue pork and avocado resembled Teddy Atsumori, squished by Ike's Datsun. It made him queasy. But, he kept this to himself. Ike and Ebb sat quietly, eating.

Back in the Datsun, Ike cut over on Washington Boulevard, through Culver City, to Higuera Street. Coming out on Rodeo Road, Ike pulled into the 7-11 at the corner of La Cienega.

"Need anything?" Ike asked.

"I'm cool," Ebb replied.

"As a breeze," Ike said, getting out.

Ebb sat, watching traffic. It was a peculiar day.

Ike returned with a pack of cigarettes, and a lighter. He made a left, back onto Rodeo. Tossing the pack's plastic, outer wrapping out the window, he pulled two cigarettes. He lit one. The other, he handed to Ebb.

"Quit smoking?" Ike asked.

"I thought you did," Ebb replied.

"I did," Ike said. "Want one?"

"Sure."

Ike let go of the wheel, leaned over and with one hand lit the cigarette, the other covering the flame.

"Thanks," Ebb said.

Ebb wondered where they were going, but he kept this to himself. He'd kept a lot of things to himself over the past hour.

Ike made a right on Somerset. Near the corner of Coliseum Street, they saw Harry Chikubushima's car jacked up on his driveway, Harry's signature overall pant legs sticking out from under, amongst a scattering of tools. Ike pulled to the side of the road, and got out.

"Harry?" Ebb heard Ike call out.

"Yeah?" came a voice from under the car.

Ike picked up a wrench and smacked both Harry's knees. A muffled scream came from under the car. Ebb calmly dragged his cigarette in the passenger seat, watching the legs squirm. Ike gave the car a couple shoulder nudges until the jack toppled, and the car dropped atop Harry. The legs stilled. Ike got back in the car.

"Let's go see Jane," Ike said, pulling away.

"Alright," Ebb replied.

Jane Aoi was an old neighborhood friend. She lived in a Bronson Avenue apartment across from Crenshaw Square, just a few blocks from Harry Chikubushima. In spite of the day, Ebb knew no harm was coming at this next stop. Jane was a sweetie. Perhaps, Ebb thought, Ike needed her comforting demeanor to assuage whatever anguish disposed him toward his recent calamities.

Ike parked around the corner, on 39th Street, and they walked the half block back to Jane's building. Ike knocked.

"Hey, boys," Jane greeted them with a tilt-headed smile. "Come on in."

The place was strewn with books. Jane was currently in the Master's Degree program for Spanish Literature, at U.C.L.A.

"Sorry for the mess… well, you know I'm not but hell, you know what I mean," she grinned. "Have a seat! Let me get you some tea."

Ike and Ebb plopped on the couch, while Jane walked into the kitcheonette to brew a pot of hot water.

"So, whatcha boys up to today?"

"Nothin' much," Ike said.

"Got some hamburgers for lunch," Ebb said. "Sorry we didn't bring you any… well, you know we're not, but you know what I mean," he smiled.

"Just out enjoying a lazy California Saturday," Ike continued.

Jane came back with a pot of tea, a bag of Japanese crackers, and went back for cups. She returned, poured, slid a stack of books blocking an end table drawer, opened it, pulled out a baggie of marijuana and a pipe. She began packing the pipe.

"I was up all night, reading. Pretty exciting Friday night, huh? I don't know about some of these books they got us on; some of them are pretty gay. But, you know, if I wanna pipe, I gotta pay. Shit, was that right? I dunno, you know what I mean," she said, passing Ike the first hit.

Ike dragged the pipe and passed it to Ebb. Ebb dragged and passed it to Jane. Jane to Ike. Ike to Ebb. Ebb to Jane.

"Thing is," said Ike with a contemplative pause, "I've been thinking about trading in my car. What do you guys think?"

Ebb was too amused to reply.

"I dunno," said Jane. "I kinda like it. Don't see them around too often, anymore. Kinda matches your personality, Ike. You're a rare breed, yourself."

"H'yeah," Ike harumphed. "I kinda feel I'm mileaging out myself, though. Can I trade myself in?"

They all laughed.

Ebb picked up a book and began reading. It was in Spanish.

"Where the hell did you come up with Spanish Literature?" Ebb asked.

"I dunno, I spent a couple years in Spain and liked it. It's a beautiful country," Jane said.

"I didn't know you spoke Spanish," said Ike.

"Picked up enough while I was there. There's something soothing about the language. Came back and started reading, and thought I'd take some classes."

Only Jane, thought Ebb. Take off to Spain on a whim, come home, read a few books and qualify for "some classes" in an accredited foreign language Master's Degree program. Ike never finished high school, and Ebb dropped out during his second semester of college. Jane's intellect, thought Ebb, was worth more than the two of them combined.

Ike excused himself to the bathroom. Jane looked at Ebb.

"Is he doing okay?" she asked.

"Okay as can be, I guess," Ebb replied.

"I kind of worry about him, sometimes," Jane concernedly whispered. "He seems tense. Like there's a lot on his mind."

"He took me to Mago's for a hamburger, this afternoon. Wouldn't let me pay. I'd say there's a lot on his mind."

"Haha, you know what I mean."

Ebb looked at Jane.

"I think you know what I mean, too. No es de hablar," Ebb tried in broken Spanish. "Olvidas."

"Te entiendo."

Ike returned, thanked Jane, and said he had to be going. He gave Jane a soft kiss on the forehead. Ebb gave her a hug in the doorway, and she waved them off down the driveway.

Ebb pulled the handle of the 280z, but it was locked.

"I gotta go," said Ike. "Come over here a sec."

Ebb walked around the car. Ike reached in, grabbing the wrench and cigarettes.

"Here, I quit smoking." He held up the wrench. "Need a crescent?"

"I could use one. A lighter, too."

"Oh."

Ike reached back in the car for the lighter, and handed it to Ebb. He took a moment into Ebb's eyes, then snatched Ebb into a growling, pounding hug.

"Thanks for lunch, man," said Ebb.

"Anytime. Catchu later."

Ebb watched Ike Sekidera's Datsun 280z disappear down 39th Street. Then he walked back to Jane's, to ask for a ride home.

EDREN T. SUMAGAYSAY

Chapter Five: Timing Is Everything

She wore that red coat he loved to hug. He danced with it, every night, when she went to work. Totally naked. And that's the truth.

"You're late," she says, looking pissed.

"I know," he says, parachuting his baggy black slacks across from her in the outdoor booth. "But timing is everything, right?"

'Twas 3 in the morning. At one of those open all night if you're Korean or with a Korean, Korean Coffee Houses, entrenched in one of the many millions of strip malls in Korea Town, Los Angeles, California, during a brisk, very early morning winter. The place was called White, and it found itself cradled between the *No Ri Bong*, which still thumped with singing drunkards, and the Vu's Nail Salon, which wasn't a nail salon because it was still open. If you know what I mean.

He found her waiting for him in the smoking patio. A good spitting distance from the cars drunkenly whizzing by on the Saturday night/Sunday morning street. In one hand, a cup of coffee, in the other, her cell phone.

"Well, Reggie's coming," she says, looking past him, taking a sip of coffee from the smooth ceramic cup. "You said you weren't going to be here. So I asked him to come, instead."

"I changed my mind, Sweetheart," he says, smiling. "Makes for good writing after the fact, don't you think?"

She rolls her eyes. "You know this is going to end up badly, don't you? You do realize this? He's been drinking all night and if he sees you sitting here with me, God knows what he's likely to do to you."

"Hey, Pumpkin, if he sees me, he sees me." He pulls out his pack of cigarettes, his wallet, his cell phone, and one stick of chewing gum, and places them on the table. "If he's as drunk as I think he is, then he'll see four of me and re-think the entire ass whoopin'."

"Want a cup of coffee?" she asks, already waving down the efficiently dressed waiter. She mouths something to him in Korean. He nods and makes his way to the back.

"Did you ask him to make it extra awesome?" he says, lighting up a cigarette. He takes a couple of quick puffs and then hands it to her. "Here you go, Darlin'. I inhaled all the nicotine and chemicals out for you. Just pure tobacco now."

106

"No. I ordered it extra retarded," she says, accepting the cigarette. She takes a puff between her round, red lips, fruitlessly trying to push down a smile.

"Damn it…" she whispers.

"What was that, Baby?" He catches the smile. "Was that a little smile? Are my jokes working on you? You no longer immune to my awesomeness?" He smiles, himself. "Self-high-five!" After he gives himself a self-high-five, he pulls out another cigarette, for himself this time, and lights it up, burning with satisfaction.

"No." She lets herself smile. "You jerk face." She lets go of her mock-anger. Then she lets herself laugh. He joins her. They look at each other, happy to be around each other. Finally, both warm up. It's nice. "I didn't think you would show up," she says, pouting, leaning towards him, fingertips massaging her neck. "I mean, I had a feeling you would, but I really thought you weren't going to come. You said you weren't coming. Why did you come?"

"I had to, Strawberry Cherry." He looks at her strawberry cherry red lips. The ones that look extra sweet in pout mode. "I can't stay away from a good thing."

She smiles, while rolling her eyes. "Now *that* was a funny joke." She takes a puff of her cigarette and exhales into the cool, 3 a.m., strip-mall-lit air.

He smiles. She smiles. Back and forth, back and forth. Towards each other. And closer.

His coffee comes. He temporarily breaks from her consuming gaze, and grabs three creamers and four packets of sugars. Pours them in, one by one. Stirs 20 times to the right, waits until the coffee whirlpool subsides into stillness. Then stirs 20 times to the left. He waits for the movement to stop once again. Finally, he takes a sip.

His eyes widen happy. "Nice," he says.

"Why do you do that?" she asks, perplexed. "That little weird little coffee ritual thing you do? You do it every time. Every single time. Why do you do that?"

"It tastes better this way," he says, taking another satisfying sip.

"Really?" she asks.

"Yeah," he says. "Wanna try?"

She shrugs her shoulders. "Okay."

She sips. Puts the cup down. Looks at him. "Tastes the same to me."

He smiles. "Well, that's because you didn't put in the work."

She lets out a tiny giggle, through a tinier smile. "I get it."

"Now you know why I had to come, right, Sweetie Pie?" he winks.

"I suppose," she says coyly. She takes a sip of her coffee, puffs on her cigarette, pulls out her cell phone, and begins to text. In that order.

"What're you doing?" he asks, trying to look over the table. "Who are you texting, Gold Medalist?"

"Gold Medalist?" she asks puzzled, unable to help from smiling without breaking her texting flow.

"I dunno," he shrugs. "I couldn't think of anything else..." He attempts to correctly guess which letters are being pressed, according to her finger movements and the positioning of the keypad. "Damn, you text pretty fast."

"Gold Medalist," she smiles.

Smiles does he, as well.

"I'm texting, Reggie," she says, entering the zone. "Telling him not to come."

"Woo hoo!" He raises his arms in victory.

"Don't celebrate yet, Flash," she says. "We still got until morning. You still have to impress me."

He cocks his head to the side, smiles a crooked smile.

She finally puts her phone away, cocks her head to the same side. Takes one last puff of her cigarette, and flicks it into the street. His eyes lock on hers, and hers accept his. They slowly memorize the shapes on their faces. How beautiful.

"Okay, buddy." She puts her forearms on the table, leans towards him and demands, "Tell me some stories, Xavier. And they better be good, Mister. It's getting cold."

Chapter Seven: See, They Say

Perfect isn't going to happen. A happy looking guy and a happy looking girl having a happy looking time. This upsets the Natural Order of things. Millions of tiny imperfections surrounding his life are going to make damned well sure this happy looking bubble is going to burst, or in the very least, float too far away to keep safe. It has to be this way. Natural Order of things, they say.

To keep Anna Lisa Kristina happy, he has to be sad. That's just the way it is.

"You look sad," Janie notices.

"How can you tell? I'm wearing sunglasses," Xavier responds.

"Yeah, I kind of noticed that," she replies. "At 3 in the morning."

"Well, coffee around this time doesn't make sense either, does it, Angel," he says.

"Well, unless you want to stay up to watch the sunrise, it makes perfect sense," she says, folding her arms, sitting back in her chair, smiling, daring him to continue the repartee.

"Well, Princess, that's why I'm wearing the sunglasses," he says, folding his arms, sitting back in his chair, exactly like she. "It's for the sunrise." He winks.

"Well," she says, satisfied with the riposte, wanting it to go even further, "how can you see the sunrise with those sunglasses on?"

"I'll see it just fine," he says.

"No you won't. You'll see it through some dim, filtered, version of what the sunrise should look like."

"Actually, depends on which eye I'm looking through."

"What do you mean?"

"I'm left-handed."

"What does that mean?"

"It means my left eye is stronger."

"That's retarded."

"No, that's anti-retarded. It's retarded retardant."

"You're so stupid," she laughs, giving in.

"No, I took an internet IQ test and I got a 150, suckah!" he boasts. "That makes me totally not stupid." He winks, enjoying the pulsating banter.

She smiles. He smiles, hoping this will last a little longer. Any moment, he's expecting to hear the inevitable 'pop'.

"But seriously, Xavier, what's up with the sunglasses?" she asks, extending her cigarette smoking fingers, expectantly, towards him.

"Hey, I got a wild idea. I'm going to change the subject." He reaches into his shirt pocket again, pulls out two cigarettes, places them both in between his lips, and lights them both with one dexterous motion. He hands her one, inhales the remaining one in his mouth, and immediately exhales while asking, "Do you think people will ever get smart?"

She takes a drag of her cigarette, oh so daintily. "Sure. Why not. You call it evolution, right? Isn't that what people do anyway? Evolve?"

"Yeah, but I think people are too scared to let it happen," he says, taking another quick drag of his cigarette. "They like things the way they are. They don't understand it's supposed to change."

"What are you babbling about?" she asks while signaling the waiter to bring her their check. He nods.

"Take that dude over there in the corner, right?" he says, pointing with his chin towards a slight looking fellow. Sad, curly, crown for hair, slouched shoulders, seemingly about to drown himself in his cup of coffee. "That guy is a classic hopeless romantic fuck."

"How can you tell?"

"Because he's by himself, drinking coffee at 3 in the morning, in a corner."

"How does that make him a hopeless romantic fuck? He could be just some dude who's too drunk to drive home and needs a couple of minutes to detox."

"Well, I also know him. That's, Corn. The Corn I've been telling you about. The one who's in love with his best friend. For ten years. Never told her. Because she's always had a boyfriend. Never thought it was appropriate. Never wanted to rock her boat. Mister quintessential best friend. Who's in love."

"Well, what does that have to do with people evolving, or whatever you call it?" Janie asks, almost humoring Xavier's strange conversational direction. She enjoys flirting more than trying to figure out the world. The entire game of subtlety, innuendo, and imagination. That is her cup of coffee.

But Xavier's cute. And he tells funny jokes. He helps her forget about her problems. She is also fully aware of this bubble they find themselves in. However, unlike him, she relishes in the
110

ephemeral. It makes her feel alive. And, for her, with everything going on in her life, this is what she needs. More than ever.

So she'll sit there, wait for him to finish trying to figure everything out, because when he comes back, he is so much fun to play with.

The waiter arrives with their check. Janie pulls a credit card from her purse and hands it to him. He quickly bows and walks towards the register, to ring them up.

Xavier takes a drag. "He's stayed in 'The Friend Zone' for the past ten years."

"Well, what if she doesn't like him back?" Janie points out.

"Doesn't matter. Death is inactivity. Life is movement. It's the process of Evolution. That's why poetry is stupid."

"What the hell are you talking about?" She can't help but laugh.

Xavier exhales a string of smoke. He looks Janie dead in the eye and says, "Corn just sits there, writes poetry, about his love, this beautiful thing, his best friend, out of reach, unrequited. But he doesn't really do anything about it. He takes no actual action. Now, if he told her, or did something uber-romantic to woo her, like write a book for her, or paint her naked face on the side of a building or some stupid shit like that, and even if she didn't feel the same way, he would've done something about it; he would've, literally, taken action, and, thus, the molecules would be prepared to jump to the next speed, the next evolutionary step.

"But because he has no testicles, those molecules are just waiting. Sitting there. Idle. They're not moving. They're inactive. So they die. And then he dies.

"Baby Rainbow," he says, flicking his cigarette out onto the street, accidentally hitting a car passing by, "it may seem the most beautiful, hopelessly romantic stuff of tear-jerking movies and great romance novels, but that kind of story is just plain retarded because it all leads to the same thing." He sighs. Looks at Corn, poor, poor, sweet Corn. "The guy dies in the end."

She looks at him, sympathetically. He seems to be speaking from experience.

He catches her concerned glance. Xavier shrugs his shoulders, adjusts his sunglasses, and puts on a big smile.

"You're so weird," she says. This is her opportunity to shift the conversation back. "But that's what I like about you." The waiter returns with the receipt. She signs it; he bows and walks away, content with the tip.

"What about my bulging biceps?" Xavier says, rapidly raising his eyebrows for confirmation.

"No. Because that is retarded, you bastard." She smiles, getting her things ready. "Let's go?"

"Am I driving?" he asks, getting up.

"Yup," she says, handing him her car keys. "My car."

"Sweet," he says. "Sunrise, here we come."

Chapter Eleven: So Ad Infinitum

After the Parking Lot Incident and the High-Speed, Angry, Drunk, Newly Ex-Boyfriend Chase around Korea Town, they decided to watch the sunrise at McGrath State Beach, on the outskirts of Oxnard, California. A good hour's drive from Pasadena, where the motorcycle police escorted them.

It was time for the krill to glow their fluorescent blue. The full moon was scheduled to make an appearance in the middle of the ocean's dark, morning sky. And McGrath was far enough for the both of them to hide from everything they didn't feel like dealing with.

A few hours is all they really needed. It is all they expected.

He is driving, smoking a cigarette and drinking gas station coffee. She is sleeping, curled like a cat in the passenger seat. They go up the 101 freeway. Windows slightly cracked, enough for cigarette smoke to leave their tiny bubble. Heater on full blast so she'll be comfortable. Somewhere in the quiet he listens to the tapping of wheel against freeway, her uneven breathing, and his own bouncing thoughts.

Xavier loves chubby cheeks. Just goes nuts for them. Absolutely adores them. Something adolescent about them. Something unfinished. And he loves unfinished things.

Janie is as unfinished as a person could get without receiving legal government help. Not to say she's completely helpless, but that she purposely places herself in situations where another person's help is the only thing that can keep her from killing herself. She attracts sympathy and clings to it. She relies on it. She doesn't know any other kind of life.

It makes perfect sense she finds herself flying in the dead of night with a guy who's just as dependent on excuses. Because they're both stupid. Just like everyone else who doesn't accept the rule of Evolution.

"This is a long ass drive," he thinks to himself. "I guess this is where I start talking to myself."

He looks at, Janie. "You know, you sleep with an angry face. Must be your dreams. Or maybe it's just how you are. Maybe you got issues, maybe you got excuses. Maybe that's why you'd meet me at an all night coffee spot, go away with me to see the sunrise, all the while, your newly ex-boyfriend is wondering where you are. Now you're with me. I wonder why.

"Ya know I can't even hug without feeling guilty? It makes me feel weird, touching other people. I don't know, but somewhere deep down inside, I feel like I shouldn't. Like it's wrong. All the while, some sort of hole keeps getting bigger and bigger. And I figure, things like this, people like you, for the most part, help me forget.

"Do you see what I'm saying, Janie? Do you understand what I'm talking about when I talk about people being scared to move? To jump to the next level of their Evolution? I'm not just saying that to sound like an asshole. I'm saying it because it's really fucking hard to do. And it takes a brave motherfucker to do something like that. Me, I don't got the courage. I'm just as scared as Corn. As scared as you."

He reaches out his hand to her sleeping one. He grabs it, almost waking her up with his fearful grip. "I wonder what's going to happen once our toes dig into the cold, silver sand. Stare out into that panoramic ocean, lit by the full moon and the glowing krill. Are we going to hold each other as insignificant pieces to a giant reason why everything is the way it is? Are we going to feel less than mortal and kiss away our fears? As a way to numb ourselves? So we won't feel like we have to move? So we don't have to change? So those things that bother us, about us, can look like something else?

"I wonder if this big illusion, this pretty, little, bubble we've made, I wonder if we can find a way to keep it away from everything. Because, if it takes courage to pop it, and move on, I don't think I got the testicles.

"Fucking shit, man. I'm pretty fucked in the head. I got issues."

Xavier laughs to himself. "Issues beget issues beget issues, and so ad infinitum…"

Janie begins to wake up. Slowly, groggy. Wiping the sleep from her round face. "Are we there yet?" she whispers.

"Yes," he says, easily slipping back into his role in this fucked up love story. "I wanna bite off your cheeks. Very hard."

"Wow." She smacks her mouth awake. "That was very romantic."

"Hey, Songbird," Xavier says. "We're here!"

"Xavier…" Janie says. "Why are we holding hands?"

"Well, while you were asleep, you were having these hot dreams of me. Your unconscious hand grabbed mine. I tried to pry myself free, but to no avail. You're pretty strong, Janie." He smiles.

She smiles. The same smiles that have helped cover up scars the entire morning.

Xavier exits the 101, follows the signs to the trail that leads to the McGrath campgrounds, finds a good parking spot, a good 100 yards from the beach head, and, finally, parks.

"We walk from here," he says. "Bring your jacket. It's going to be cold."

She reaches into the backseat and grabs her red jacket. That same beautifully smooth red jacket, that red jacket he loves seeing her wear. "Are you ready for some fun?" she asks, wryly.

"With you?" he says. "Always."

He smiles. She smiles.

They get out, walk to the beach, hand in hand, moon lighting half their faces, while the ocean waits to wash everything away.

Chapter Fifteen: Waves Crash Blue Dreams

Simple wave upon simple wave comes lapping on the beach shore with every breath they take, synchronizing almost. A luminescent blue trapped inside each one of the waves. The krill glowing. It looks surreal. Right out of a movie.

Moon in full radiance creating silver half-masks on their faces. Perfect costumes for this early morning. Perfect accessories to the characters they play.

It's a beautiful scene, regardless. Basic and epic, at the same time.

Wrapped tightly together, sharing a poncho bought in Mexico three months earlier, a dark haired man and a chubby cheeked woman sit as insignificant participants in this large, panoramic, picture. Chin nuzzles neck, lips occasionally peck, and eyelashes flutter on earlobes.

"You know, that's krill," states the man.

"What's krill?" asks the woman.

"The blue glow," the man responds.

"Duh," giggles the woman. "I'm asking what krill is."

"Oh. Ha," smiles the man. "They're kind of like plankton. A step higher. Basic building block of the food chain."

"Why do they glow?" she asks.

"Because they have this body part that can emit light," he says. "Some people say it's to make it harder for predators to see them."

"So glowing bright blue makes them harder to see?" She half smiles. "No wonder they're at the bottom of the food chain."

He smiles. Then lets out a deep, deep, sigh, holding her tighter. "Well, when you think about it, the world of the ocean is a lot different than ours. When these creatures look up, all they can see is this shimmering light from what they would consider their sky. It's either the sun or the reflection off the moon, depending on if it's day or night. So if the krill were to glow, it would actually disguise them better. Them predators would look up, and see a lot of light. And that's all they would see. A lot of light."

"I don't get it," she frowns coquettishly. "Kiss me again, you fool!"

Her soft cheek receives the warm kiss of the man holding her. This man makes her feel bright.

He isn't like the others. He isn't like her, as of a few hours ago, newly ex-boyfriend. He made her feel bad. Like an outcast. Like she was wrong to exist. Like she didn't belong.

This man, Xavier, however, understands her. He lets her be. This man accepts her. And that's all she had ever wanted in a relationship with a man. Something simple. Something basic. Just hug, cuddle, kiss, and be on his merry way, so she can do the things she likes to do when she's alone. What she's always wanted in a relationship, is to not be in a relationship.

This man is perfect. For the time being. She knows it. She accepts it. Heck, she prefers it. Janie is one of the few people in the world who feels relieved when she hears the 'pop.'

They kiss for the millionth time. Lines on lips match. Flawless pressure. Faces no longer exist. It is one shared breath. And it's in perfect harmony with the gentle rhythm of the waves sounding in the still-dark morning.

"I... I...," she begins. "Xavier... I want to tell you something."

He closes his eyes. Takes one long, deep, inhale. Waits. Then exhales. He hugs her tight. Bottom lip tickling her earlobe.

"Mmmm...," she mmms.

He wants to forget. She doesn't want him to.

"Xavier...," she whispers. "You're my best friend..."

He opens his eyes. His breathing becomes short. He loosens his hold on her. His muscles tense. She can't tell, wrapped up in her own intentions.

"I just wanted to let you know that. You have a special place in my heart," she says. "You never judge me, even after all the fucked up things I've done. I mean, c'mon, let's face it, I'm always messing things up no matter how hard I try not to. But you, you're always there for me when I need you. You make me laugh, you make me think. You are the best partner in crime anyone can hope to have. And I do, Xavier. I love you."

She turns her head to his. Purses her lips and closes her eyes. She leans in close for their millionth and one kiss. And she is lost again. She smiles, appreciative of this sedative.

His thoughts scramble. The glowing blue waves, the human body heat, the soft sand, the full moon, the fact they are miles away from home, metaphorically, on the edge of the earth, all of these medicated, romantic, reasons why they left the world behind in the first place, dissolve once she says the words, 'You're my best friend.' Because, after that, all he can think about is Anna Lisa Kristina.

He hears the 'pop.' The bubble is broken. Everything around him gets colder.

Janie's body, slowly, with purpose, starts rubbing against his hug. She purrs. She exposes her neck. Her fingers lace his, tighter with every passing second. Just like before, she knows how to get what she wants from him. It's so easy when there's no defense. No strength.

"Xavier...," she moans.

"...yeah...," he whispers, easily intoxicated.

"I want to fuck again..." She turns her body, overpowering his lips with hers. He accepts. She has her way. They both linger in the manifestations of these quixotic moments.

He thinks to himself, 'This is some fucked up shit. I'm one fucked up individual. What the fuck is the fucking matter with me? What the fuck is a matter with the both of us?'

Her hands find and trace the outlines of his chest. Her lips travel from mouth to neck to collarbone.

He drowns in her overwhelming affection, once again, temporarily forgetting about Anna Lisa Kristina.

Chapter Sixteen: Dumb

He is dreaming. About a time, long, long, ago, when the world was perfect.

He was an immortal, invulnerable, twenty-something adventurer. Sure he was in debt up to his eyeballs, and sure he had no permanent place to live, and sure he drove a car with a broken window, but he had Anna Lisa Kristina. His best friend. The love of his life. No amount of fucked up, real world, adult, shit could ever make him unhappy as long as she was on the other side of that phone or coffee table or restaurant booth. She was the only person in the world who could make him feel human. Who could make him feel like he deserved better. The only person who could make him move.

They were riding on the back of a silver dragon named Maxwell, on their way to the Monastery of Light, high atop the Thunderdome Mountains, to join the monks in the annual Ceremony of Dialogue. Her arms were tightly wrapped around his waist, his hands holding onto the neck of Maxwell for support.

Wind blowing through both their hairs, the world below them looking like a toy, the sun just out of reach, flying through cotton candy clouds. It was friggin' awesome. Dreams have a way of feeling like that.

"Howdy doo dee, Dumb," she asked with a wry smile. "Howdy doo dee."

That was Anna Lisa Kristina. Chubby cheeks, shoulder length hair, glasses, and red, round lips. Easily mistaken for a Korean, but she was Pilipino.

"I'm fine, Kris," he replied. "Just don't let go of me. Maxwell is on his medication."

"If, for some reason, I fall, I'm taking you with me, Dumb." She tickled him.

"As usual, I'll probably follow," he said. "Because I'm a dumb ass."

She rested her head in between his shoulder blades. "That's what I love about you, Dumb. Your dumb ass-edness." He could feel her smile.

"Say, Kris," he began. "I wanna ask you something."

"I swear, Dumb, if this is another one of your 'why do cats and dogs hate each other' kind of questions, I'm gonna throw you off of Maxwell!"

"Ha. No. It's more personal."

"Well, that makes it more comfortable, now doesn't it?"

"I'm serious. I want to ask you a question."

"Alrighty. Shoot. I'm all yours."

He gulped. Took a minute to collect his thoughts. Then he let out a deep breath.

"Have you ever thought about you and me, ya know, becoming more than just friends?"

Her hands quickly let go of his waist. He could feel her slipping. He turned to see what was going on, to try to catch her, to try to keep her safe, but it was too late. She was falling. And he couldn't reach her. She was saying something, but he couldn't make out the words. All he could do was watch her fall farther and farther away from him.

"MAXWELL!" he yelled. "We gotta catch her!"

"No can do, mon ami," Maxwell said. "We've got a schedule to keep."

"What the fuck, dude!" Xavier frantically said, watching his best friend fall farther and farther away. "She's gonna die!"

"Well, that's your fault, bro," said Maxwell. "I'm not changing course one bit, suckah!"

Anna Lisa Kristina's body plummeted closer to the ground, faster with every second. Xavier watched in horror. He couldn't do anything from the back of Maxwell.

So he jumped.

She was mouthing words that he couldn't understand. He tried swimming through air to get closer to her, but that didn't help. The harder he tried, the faster she fell. The more effort he exerted, the more he screamed, the more he demanded, the farther she went. Eventually, she was so far away from him, he couldn't even see her anymore.

He started crying. Feeling so alone. Helpless. Guilty. Falling. Nothing to hold on to. No one around. No longer.

Then he wakes up. Breathing heavy, perspiring. Sand clutched in his hand.

He looks around. The ocean in front of him. The morning sun. A poncho. A sleeping woman right next to him. Someone who wasn't Anna Lisa Kristina.

"This is some fucked up shit, man," he says to himself. "This is some fucked up shit…"

He blinks. He can feel tears. He wipes them away. He sees the waves sliding onto the shore. The sun, high in the sky. He looks at his watch and it says, 9:35AM.

The sunrise came and went. He didn't get a chance to see it. He was asleep. Dreaming of things.

Things that came and went.

Things that come and go.

Things he'll never have again.

Things that made him feel normal.

He closes his eyes tight. Clenches his fist. Grits his teeth. Frowns. Gives himself 60 seconds for pity. That's all he is going to give himself. That's all he can afford, nowadays.

When he finishes, he gets back into character. He looks around for his sunglasses. Wipes the sand off of them. Puts them on. This helps.

He looks around for his pack of cigarettes and his lighter. Finds them in his shirt pocket. There are three left.

He lights up one of the cigarettes and, just like everything else in his life, does his best to forget.

VICKY LUU

When You Pull Over Late at Night

"How much?" Greg leaned over to the passenger side, his window halfway down. He stared at a gorgeous blond; long legs, tight dress, accentuating all the right parts for Greg. He was a lonely guy.

"Excuse me?" Debbie flipped her head back, her blond wig slightly more evident.

"How much?" Greg said just a little bit louder.

"How much what, motherfucker?" Debbie stepped closer to Greg's vehicle and leaned up against the window.

"C'mon, stop playing around. I know...I know where I am." Greg tried to hold his confidence, show that he was no stranger to the underbelly of his town, but who was he trying to kid.

"And just where are you, motherfucker?" Debbie adjusted her purse.

"Look, if I pay you extra, would you tone down the potty mouth? And I'm kind of in a hurry."

"Say what? Who you think you is, motherfucker? Or more importantly, who do you think I am?" In the latter half of that statement, Debbie's voice dropped a little deeper.

Greg rolled his window all the way down. He stared at Debbie, her face this time. His eyes widened.

"...Scott?" Greg croaked out.

"That's right, motherfucker. Now get the fuck out of here," Scott spoke, back to Debbie-voice.

Greg wasn't sure what to make of the situation, as Scott was his supervisor. He slowly rolled up the passenger side window.

"And don't be late again to work, motherfucker," Scott said as he walked away from Greg's car.

Greg sat for a moment. He decided, then, that it was time to get his life back on track. He would rejoin the gym tomorrow, and actually go.

When They Suddenly Decide to Leave

He drove all night. In his mind his destination was clear, but to others it seemed ludicrous and irresponsible. He left only a few goodbye letters, only vaguely explaining his actions. He wrote to his older brother, his youngest cousin, and his favorite aunt.

Those who did not receive a letter were offended, to say the least, and very hurt. Not only was his leave of absence uncalled for, to them, but it created a series of accusations to everyone in the family who may have been responsible. Or, maybe, to those who should have been more responsible.

He drove, for several nights, all the way to the East Coast. Perhaps to find himself, to find someone, to find something. No one really knows. But he returned, a year and a half later, apologized for leaving so suddenly, and for so long, and immediately got himself a job.

He paid back all the money he had borrowed from family members and friends. Seemingly, he had decided to put his life back on track. Yet those who never received a letter, and were told not to read the ones that were written, will never really learn what happened out there on that road. And will never know why he left in the first place. And will never understand how childhood so quickly escaped them.

When You Sit in the Car Outside of a Friend's Place

"You're holding your breath again."

"What? No, I'm not."

Cliff exhaled. He reached up to grab his chest and realized the pain that was there. Perhaps he had been holding his breath. He was known for doing this whenever he was extremely nervous. Other things Cliff did when he was nervous were: biting his lower lip until it bled a little, flaring his nostrils, cleaning his glasses constantly, and rubbing the insides of his feet together.

Thom reached over and placed his hand on top of Cliff's. Thom knew all of Cliffs' nervous habits by now. The only ones he found endearing were the feet rubbing and the nostril flaring. Otherwise, he urged Cliff to try and keep the other ones under control. Thom's only nervous habit was to say out loud that he was nervous.

"You're making me nervous," Thom said as he squeezed Cliff's hand.

"I'm sorry." Cliff took a few deep breaths. "I can't help it."

"It's not so bad. You'll see," Thom tried to say reassuringly, but the uncertainty was there.

"I believe that you believe that there's nothing to worry about. And I want that too, you know that, but it's too hard to well... believe." Cliff caught himself thinking too much about his own words. He didn't like the way he was sounding, but couldn't help himself. Five years ago he had started sounding more and more like his mother. As much as Cliff wanted to change that, he knew he couldn't. Inherently, he was a worrier.

Thom decided to take the initiative and, once again, be the motivator. "I'm going to say it one more time, and then I'm never going to say it again, and if you don't believe me this time, I won't know what else to do and we're never going to do this again."

He took in a breath, looked straight ahead and said sternly. "We *will* win this Pictionary tournament."

Kaila – '89 Grey Toyota Pickup

She smashed it all into a million pieces. Too many for her to pick up and put back together. Too tiny for her to see what used to be so clear.

Kaila opened her hand and let the desecrated crumbs of her prescribed anti-depressants fall onto her pale blue jeans. She no longer wanted to take them. She realized that the idea of having to take these pills for her depression was only making her more depressed.

Kaila wiped her hand on the empty passenger side. She quickly grabbed a cigarette out of her shirt pocket and lit that motherfucker up. The car filled with smoke before Kaila let open a small crack in the window. She then watched the smoke carefully escape, slipping by her and vanishing into the outside.

Her eyes landed on a girl in a green Jetta. She immediately saw something she wished she could shout, like some unknown future connection. Kaila believed too much in fairy tales; her own though, was not anything that had already been written.

What if, she thought, she could reach out to this mysterious girl? Maybe save her from something. An illness, Kaila decided. She would save her from an illness. She imagined herself stepping out of her car and tapping on the Jetta's window.

The door would open, and something anew would begin. Kaila likened herself to a modern day superhero, sometimes. Her only weakness, however, was her constant enamored state when being around a pretty face. Or, even, a handsome one.

Kaila looked behind her. The cabinet, which her mother had left her, was strapped down in the back, covered in a sheet Kaila used to sleep in as a child. She noticed the long scratch on the side, peeking out from under the sheet as the corners fluttered from the breeze. It happened when Kaila and her mother tried to get the desk through the front door. Afterward, her mother scolded her for not being more careful with the desk, and her life.

Kaila looked back at the girl in the green Jetta. She decided that at some point they would meet, and perhaps fall in love.

Just not today.

When We Get to the End

"The world is ending today. Quickly, get in the car."

"What are you talking about?"

"I had this dream that today, the streets would flood. Everything would be submerged, everything destroyed. Civilization ends today. That is what I dreamt."

"So? It was just a dream…"

"But my dreams always come true. I need you to get in the car, so we can drive to the only place that won't flood. So that I can save you."

"I don't need you to save me."

"Please, get into the car."

"Where is this place?"

"It's at the top."

"Top of what?"

"Just the top. I can't explain; I saw it in my dreams."

"And they always come true."

"Yes. Now, will you get in the car?"

"No."

"Why not?"

"If the world ends today, then I want to end with it. I don't want to be in this world alone, with just you."

"How can you say that?"

"Because it's the truth. I'm sorry. It's not that I don't love you, but it's just too scary a thought. To be so alone."

"But I want to save you."

"No, save yourself."

Allan G. Aquino is a poet and professor who teaches courses on Filipino and Asian American literature, history, and media at Cal State University, Northridge. His poems have been published in journals including *Tinfish* (UH), *The Northridge Review,* and *Amerasia.* By way of The Writers Workshop, he has experimented with horror/epistolary storytelling. Alongside his fellow artists, Allan continues to pursue illumination, the mystical, undeniable rhizome from which all Things grow.

Elaine Dolalas is an Anteater turned Trojan turned Bruin who was born and raised in the San Fernando Valley aka the Great One Eight. Formerly an office monkey extraordinaire for a large mortgage company, Elaine works in Higher Education and is happily trying to figure out the secret of life through writing, working within the Filipino-American/Asian American community, and most importantly avoiding cleaning her room.

Tony Francesconi is an Italian-American, Mormon, Jewish, Christian, Agnostic, skateboarder with a Bum Knee. He's in the advertising game, only for the paychecks to buy that new lighting kit.

Narinda Heng, after ten years of schooling in Orange County and a year and a half spent falling in love with Los Angeles, is exploring places she's never been, while maintaining her duties as a co-moderator of The Writers Workshop. She writes.

Tani Ikeda writes everyday.

Helen Kim discovered an irresistible desire for the written word over twenty years ago when criticizing her first-grade classmates: 1.) spelling simple words incorrectly, like "toock" 2.) for trying to be too "kool" 3.) and "I hate that new boy. He didn't listen to me." She carefully resisted these mistakes and sardonically recorded thoughts in a diary in the late 80s and continued since, in both legit and non-legit forms. She enjoys reading to little children at the public library, karaoke, reading, taking self-portraits and interspecies cuggling in her spare time. She was raised in and currently resides in Los Angeles, working in the nonprofit community.

Vicky Luu, born and raised in the Bay Area of Northern California, in a middle-sized town just shy of San Francisco, often yearned for city life and all its freedoms. Feeling too confined by living in a strict Asian household, she sought out Los Angeles for college, escape and, eventually, domestic life. Since moving, she has managed to land herself in a plethora of situations that sparked a creative flame, which almost died out if not for the introduction of the Writers Workshop. They have opened her eyes, fanned the fire, and forced (gently) her to get back to the root of it all: writing, writing, writing. So, she does. And is very thankful to do so, everyday.

Erik Matsunaga lives in Chicago.

Edren T. Sumagaysay is left-handed. A middle-child. He's a Capricorn. An INTJ. Born in the year of the Tiger. A high school dropout. He used to manage a gentlemen's club. Now, he works with children. Writing is about what you experience and explaining it so people can get it. Pretty simple, huh?

Grace Young is living it up between Irvine and Los Angeles. She loves her family and getting her nails done. She does not know what she wants to do when she grows up, but trusts destiny and all good things.

THEUNDENIABLES.ORG
(we write)